The Shimmer at Fog Cottage

Pete Worrall

Acknowledgements:

Thank you to the following people for without their help and guidance, this book would not be possible. Your support is very much appreciated.

Nadine Gillies for proofreading and advice of police procedures, and the subsequent logistical headaches trying to write around them.

Eileen Draycott for dotting the I's and crossing the T's.

Martin Worrall for proofreading and ensuring it all makes sense.

Chris Linaker for art & design direction and advice.

Also by Pete Worrall:

They Grow Upon The Eyes

The Doom Of The Hollow

The Unforeseen Children Of Olive Shipley

Goet

Thank You For The Music

All books are available on Amazon Kindle and paperback from the webshop at: www.peteworrall.com except for Goet & Thank You For The Music which are available on Kindle only.

The audio version of Goet, read by James Gillies with sfx by Martin Worrall, is available to stream from YouTube.

The audio version of They Grow Upon The Eyes, read by Mark Pitt, is available on Amazon and iTunes.

The Shimmer at Fog Cottage

November 7th

01:33am

The vision of the lock and its key was a blur. In Aaron Child's inebriated state, he jabbed the point of the key to where he felt the lock was, hoping luck was on his side and it would nestle into its home just so he could enter his. On his third try he was successful which indicated he was not as drunk as he had been on previous occasions, or last night to be frank. The wide spread of scratches around the lock could have been a reminder of tales of stupors far beyond his current condition, but they would have only been suggestions. Even though the evidence was there, his recall of such events had been lost at the bottom of many cheap student bar priced lagers. He smirked as he placed his money on the kitchen table and took a loaf from the breadbin. The fact that Aaron still had coins in his pocket and the sensibility to make a sandwich meant two things: the first, he might actually be awake early enough in the morning to pack up his things for when his parents were going to pick him up, probably around midday. In a normal context, early was usually around half past eleven, but seeing as he had not organised anything, early might have to be around eight o'clock because he did not want the nag from this Mother. The second was most of his drinking friends had already finished for the end of term and travelled home.

Aaron had left his games console on pause before he went out so he carried on with his army shooting game with half a sandwich hanging from his mouth as both of his hands were required to use the controller. Once he had reached the end of the level, he gave himself time to eat it and was about to continue the game when his mobile phone rang. He looked at the time. It was 1:33am. The phone number was just that, a number. His caller was not saved in his contacts and he certainly did not recognise the sequence of digits. Thoughts of ignoring it and letting it run to voice mail entered his head. It was probably a wrong number. Who would be phoning him in the middle of the night if it was not one of his friends, he thought? Certainly, nobody from his family would call him at such a late hour, unless it was an emergency. Could it be an emergency? Has something happened? Aaron picked up the phone and slid his finger across the screen. The call connected.

At first there was silence. Aaron listened carefully. The display on his phone was showing the line had definitely connected. "Hello?"

There was more silence before the quiet mewling of a woman crept through the ear piece.

"Hello? Who's there?" Aaron could now hear gentle breathing. The crackle of static began to break up the connection before the female voice on the other end of the phone whimpered. It was obvious she had been crying.

"I know it's coming, it has come for everyone else. Why can't we see it coming?"

Aaron Childs put down his game controller and frowned. "Who is this?"

"It's here, it's in the room with me. It must be."

"What're you talking about?"

"I am being watched, I can feel it. It knows I'm here."

"Who is this?" There was a pause. Aaron listened to the woman's quiet sobbing. "Do you need help?"

"I'm cut off."

"Cut off from where?"

The woman took a sharp intake of breath. *"Oh God."* She began to panic. *"I've seen the shimmer. How does it know I'm here?"*

"Can you tell me where you are?" The static increased, distorting the connection. "This line is very bad, can you move to a place with a better signal?"

"Fog Cottage is the only place."

"Fog Cottage?"

"You have to warn others. No one must ever come here."

"Here? Where's here?"

"I've seen them, I've seen the shimmer."

"The Shimmer? Where are you?"

The woman began to cry a little heavier as the static increased into bursts of white noise. *"It's like spiders crawling on my skin."*

"I think you've dialled the wrong number, because if this is a joke..." The static on the line seemed to explode and Aaron pulled the phone away from his ear, wincing as he mouthed an expletive. When he heard the noise slightly fade, he moved the handset closer to his ear.

"What's your name?"

Through sobs, the woman mumbled, *"Jessica Pu…"*

Aaron pulled the phone away from his ear for a second time as the dull thump that chilled his skin was followed by a shriek of pain. A second, louder thump suggested something had cracked or broken. The third strike seemed to meld with a groan, the resonance of a dying breath.

Aaron pressed the phone to his ear. The line was once more filled with static before suddenly falling into silence.

"Hello? Jessica? Jessica?" Aaron ended the call and fell back into his arm chair. He was unnerved, but his puzzled expression melted away as inebriated sleep took over. Whoever had called him, the strange woman who needed his help, would have to wait until the morning.

09:14am

Inspector George Watling yawned as he walked into the police station. On his way to his desk he was greeted by three officers from uniform of which he could recall the names of two out of the three. Each one offered a pleasant greeting and received a courteous murmur in return. He could not face a day of work and pleasantries, not just yet.

After he had lost his fifth game of solitaire in a row, he let his head fall back onto the headrest of the chair. He needed to close his tired eyes, only for a moment. He jerked awake, checked his watch and was thankful he had only drifted off for a couple of minutes. Looking back at his screen, he grimaced at his solitaire seventy-two percent loss rate but clicked 'new game' before shutting down the program when Sergeant Parker knocked on the open door. Watling beckoned him in and offered him a chair.

Parker gave a report to Watling before sitting down. "Last night's efforts for you to peruse."

Watling skimmed the document. "A man blows up his own family after nailing all the windows shut and then blames it on a goat. What madness. Where is he now?"

"St George's Hospital. He's comatose."

"It saves us having to question him today then."

"Have you eaten, Boss?"

Watling sighed and felt his stomach rumble. "Can you get me something?"

Parker nodded and stood up. "We're just waiting on the forensics report from Brendan. He said he'd be in around ten."

"Ten? The lazy arse. I've got two years on him yet I managed to get in for nine." Watling double checked his watch. "Well, almost nine."

Parker smirked and turned to leave but stopped when he reached the door. "Incidentally, Boss, uniform had a strange walk-in this morning."

"What time?"

"Just after eight."

"Why strange?"

"A kid gets a call in the middle of the night from a terrified woman."

Watling sat forward. "Where was she calling from?"

"All she said was Fog Cottage."

"Who took the query?"

"Chatham. She's on the front desk right now if you want to speak to her."

10:59am

Brendan Hammond entered the Police Station's mess room carrying a takeaway coffee in one hand and a pasta salad in the other. He paused when he saw Inspector Watling standing against the kitchen counter, his arms folded, and his face holding a look of thunder. The mug with the stewed tea bag sitting on the counter lacked the plumes of steam normally associated with a brewing drink. As soon as he had placed his pasta in the fridge and sipped on the last of his coffee, Brendan looked at the steeped bag. "You never make your own tea, everything alright, George?"

Watling lifted his head. "Brendan." He looked at his watch. "In on time I see."

"And you were in for nine I suppose."

Watling shot Brendan a furtive glance. "Of course."

"Any news on the goat man?"

"In a coma. When can I expect a forensics report? I am assuming you've been writing it up from home which is why you're late in."

"Of course," lied Brendan, pouring Watling's stewed brew down the sink. "In the twenty years I've known you, George, I've never seen you make your own drink. Something on your mind?"

Hilary Birtles's scowl entered the mess hall first, followed by her quick march to the fridge. She tutted when she realised there was not enough room to place her pot of couscous with walnuts and feta cheese, so she dumped it on someone else's sandwiches caring very little if she squashed them or not. "I had to park back of yonder, and it seems like a mile walk to the building. That's the last time we have a late start, Brendan." She acknowledged Watling with a slight nod who retorted with a thin smile.

"Mentor's prerogative, Hilary," said Brendan, sitting down at one of the mess tables. "For the privilege of a late start, the apprentice gets to drive in their boss." He winked at Watling who rolled his eyes.

Hilary mouthed the phrase, 'piss off', and started to make herself a drink.

Brendan sat back, crossed his legs and leaned an elbow on the table. "So, George, what's eating you up this morning?"

Watling unfolded his arms and slid his hands into his pockets. "Do you mean you're offering fresh ears, a different perspective and all that cobblers?"

"No, I'm just nosey."

The Inspector took a deep breath and rubbed his face with his palms. "This morning, a kid called Aaron Childs walks into this station. He can't be much younger than my lad, nineteen perhaps, still at university. He said he received a call in the middle of the night from someone he doesn't know, and that this someone sounded frightened for their life."

"Why this morning? Why not last night?"

"He was drunk and thought it was a joke. In fact, by all accounts, he was still fairly drunk this morning, because he said after his sobering brain had analysed the phone call he made his way here."

"I'm assuming you've called the number back," said Hilary.

"According to the automated message, the number is currently not in service," replied Watling.

Brendan sat upright. "What did the caller say?"

Watling slid his hands back into his trouser pockets. "To quote the kid, it was as if she was being chased and was hiding, or at least trying to hide."

"She? Where was the woman calling from?" Hilary added a splash of milk to her mug of tea. "Didn't she give any clue?"

"Fog Cottage."

Brendan frowned. "I've never heard of a Fog Cottage. Where is it?"

"It's not just where, it's what," said Watling.

Brendan shifted on the uncomfortable plastic moulded chair. "I don't understand."

Hilary blew on her hot drink, took a quick sip and sat opposite Brendan. Watling noticed she was making that face again, the smug expression that slightly pouts her lips and lifts up the nose. From the many things that irritated him about her, apart from not offering to make anyone else a drink, including those in the same room, this was the one that grated him the most and cemented his opinion that she was indeed a priggish know it all.

Hilary wiped her blouse with a flat palm, brushing away some imaginary lint, and spoke as if what she was about to say was common knowledge. "On train lines and around coastal areas, fog cottages are, or at least were, buildings kitted out for someone to bunk down in should there be a need for extra signalling duties in thick fog or reduced visibility, hence the name fog cottage. They can also be known as fog signal cottages as well, it's quite simple really."

"Surely, that system hasn't been around for years," said Brendan. "I'm surprised there are some left."

In his pockets, Inspector Watling dug his finger nails into his leg to distract his mind from thinking of a sarcastic retort to little miss conceited. "Just a few. Most of them have either been renovated into holiday cottages or torn down."

"Let me guess," said Brendan, "the ones that are still listed show no sign of a disturbance."

"The team are on it, but the ones we've managed to contact so far have not given us anything to go on. Trying to track down the owners of the others is taking longer than I would like."

"What's your next course of action?" asked Hilary.

"We're bringing the kid back in for questioning and, from what I can make out, he's telling the truth. Of course, we don't have the call recorded so we only have his word to go on."

"But you're not happy." Brendan knew his Inspector friend well. "You're worried about the 'she' element."

"The kid said her name was Jessica. The mobile number she used to call Aaron Childs is indeed registered to a Jessica Puce."

"And you've looked her up, I'm guessing."

"There aren't many in Britain called Jessica Puce, none of which have been reported missing yet, but there are three we're still trying to track down."

Hilary sipped at her tea. "Where are these three Jessicas from?"

The Inspector took a moment to remember all the locations. "Hull, Luton and Flint."

Brendan was about to speak but Hilary interjected. "Flint is our area." She sat up straight. "If this Aaron Childs walks into this station then there's a good chance this Jessica is local as well."

"He said he doesn't know a Jessica Puce," said Watling, rubbing his forehead. "She could be from anywhere."

Brendan inhaled and exhaled deeply. "But you expect the worst."

"Keep yourself available," said Watling. "We may need you."

"Why?" asked Hilary.

Watling sucked on his teeth for a moment creating a squeaking noise before speaking. "It's what she said...*It's in the room with me, how does it know where I am?*...Those were her words."

Brendan looked at Hilary and then back at Watling. "It?"

"She warned him never to go to Fog Cottage and then cut off."

Hilary frowned, "How do you mean, cut off? As in, she dropped the phone?"

Watling reiterated with a slight chagrin tone to his voice. "No, cut off."

"Yes, I know," said Hilary. "But, how do you mean, cut off? Did she drop the phone or did she end the call?"

"The phone line wasn't cut off, he said she was cut off."

"Cut off from what?" said Brendan, his forehead wrinkling.

Watling shrugged his shoulders. "All of the listed Fog Cottages are accessible, so what she said doesn't make any sense. The kid said she was frightened. But why call someone you don't know? Why not call the police?"

There was a natural break in the conversation and the Inspector shook his head, stood up straight and was about to leave when

Brendan held up his palm to stop him. He looked at Hilary who was rubbing her temples. "Hilary, what d'you know?"

There was a moment of quiet and then Hilary's expression changed to one of surprise as if she was shocked the idea had popped into her head. "Birdwatching."

Watling tutted and rolled his eyes before leaving the room.

11:23am

Watling stood over Sergeant Parker's shoulder regularly interrupting his searches for bird sanctuaries and nature reserves. Parker was a little irritated because he knew he could get the results a lot quicker without his superior asking him to click on every useless link. Normal practice would be the Boss would bark his orders and delegate, why is he getting more involved this time? Parker tried to subtly demonstrate his annoyance by clicking the mouse button a little more heavily than before, but perhaps it was too subtle as Watling remained unflinching and more interested in the wayward search results on screen.

The Inspector exhaled over Parker's ear and then tutted through frustrated teeth. "Bloody bird watching."

Parker paused his search. "Why are we looking?"

"Because of Brendan. He rates her, God only knows why, the irritating crone. It's a tenuous lead but I would love it if she's way of the mark, it might just bring her down a peg."

"I think she needs bringing down about five."

Watling puffed out his cheeks. "Brendan says she's his replacement for after his retirement. Not in my bloody station she's not."

"Is Brendan retiring early?"

"It's the first I've heard. All I know is if Hilary keeps giving us tenuous claptrap such as 'birdwatching' then I'll start having Brendan's brain examined for holes."

The screen displayed a map of the North West of England with red markers in a seemingly random pattern scattered across the region. The mouse pointer hovered over the Woolston Eyes Nature Reserve in Warrington, but Watling quickly dismissed it after he remembered the National Environment Agency had recently quarantined the area. He put his hands on his hips and straightened his back, yet he quickly leaned back over Parker's shoulder and pointed towards the marker that was placed in the blue section of the map.

"You've not clicked on that one."

"I thought it was an error." Parker placed the mouse over the marker. "Look, it's in the middle of the River Dee."

"No, no." Watling placed a palm on Parker's shoulder. He leaned further in and eyed the blue expanse that lay to the west of the Wirral. "That's the Dee Estuary. The marker is for the Hilbre Island nature reserve."

Suddenly, the door to the office opened. Officer Chatham, a fresh faced woman, spoke with youthful enthusiasm. "Inspector, I've spoken with Jessica Puce's parents."

"Which Jessica Puce?"

"The one from Flint."

"And?"

"Jessica didn't come home last night."

Watling looked back at the screen and then back at Chatham. "Bring them in."

As soon as Chatham had left the room, Parker searched the internet for Hilbre Island. His first hit caused Watling to stand up. "Email over the phone number for Wirral Country Park and then get uniform to West Kirby."

"Yes, Boss."

Watling patted Parker on the shoulder. "Look at the times of the tide. At six o'clock the Island will no longer be accessible, it'll be cut off."

13:45pm

The siren of the police Range Rover wailed like a banshee as the vehicle thundered along the M53 motorway. Inspector Watling sat grimacing in the passenger seat and eventually asked Sergeant Parker to switch off the caustic din. When the noise ceased, Watling's shoulders visibly relaxed and he picked up a map from the foot well. "I can concentrate now." He unfolded the map on his lap and then held it up in front of him for Parker to see. "West Kirby, it's on the west coast of the Wirral." The Inspector pointed at the location and Parker quickly glanced over. "Hilbre Island is about a mile across the Dee Estuary. When I rang the Wirral Country Park, they put me in touch with the island's Ranger who explained when it's low tide, you can walk across the sands but when the tide is in you have approximately a five hour wait until it goes out again."

Parker glanced over again. "So, anyone who didn't start to walk back to the shore in time will be stuck on the island." He looked at Watling before focusing his attention back to the road.

Watling placed the map back onto his lap. "Or be washed out to sea if they only got half way."

The Inspector took a piece of paper from the inside pocket of his coat. "Low tide is at twenty past twelve so we should be able to cross. High tide is at ten past six this evening, but at just after three o'clock, the tide will start to come back in. The Ranger explained it was too dark to cross over at low tide this morning and he's waiting until this afternoon before he travels over for his regular visit, which could be the reason why we've not heard anything about Jessica Puce."

"Or it could be that Jessica Puce is not on Hilbre Island."

Watling checked his watch; it was a quarter to two. "The island also has a fog cottage, presumably for coastal fog and mist." His phone rang but he did not speak when he answered it except for his usual greeting and a 'thank you' to complete the call. "That was the Coast Guard; they've taken one of their boats to do a recce. They can see a body on the East side. Uniform are at West Kirby already, they'll make sure no one takes a stroll over. I'll ring for an ambulance. It looks like we'll need one."

13:57pm

The only commotion at West Kirby beach was from a couple of frustrated American tourists and a few members of the marine club whose car parking spots were taken by several police cars and an ambulance. For some reason Watling was expecting quite the British kerfuffle with a crowd of tutting locals standing around with their arms folded mumbling about how much they would have been inconvenienced should they want to visit Hilbre Island even if they did not want to go. He exited the vehicle and looked out at the Wirral peninsula. The day was grey, dull, breezy and the visibility was poor, but he could just determine the shapes of three islands a little over a mile away across the sands. It did not take much of Watling's imagination to envisage the pummelling such a remote location would receive from the elements. From the car park, he could not see any of the island's buildings, and it would have been easy to doubt whether any buildings on the island actually existed. Who would want to build anything on such a location and for what purpose, he thought? Even though he knew the buildings were indeed there, standing looking from the mainland, it seemed unlikely. A car pulled up behind him and he watched Brendan and Hilary exit the vehicle. Watling looked at Hilary, and although he found her annoying, he acknowledged her intuition by simply saying, "Birdwatching."

Hilary nodded and opened the boot of the car, removing two large cases. "Hilbre Island, I don't remember my brother mentioning it, just about being 'cut off' from somewhere."

"Even so," interrupted Brendan, "a good suggestion. Inspector, what do we know?"

The wind flurried around them causing Watling to zip up his coat. "There's a body on the eastern side of the island. The rocks prevented the Coast Guard from taking a proper look."

The ranger, accompanied by a uniformed officer, approached the Inspector and greeted Watling. "Ranger Dawson, Inspector. We spoke on the phone." The six foot, unshaven man offered his hand. Watling took it. "This is my forensic team, Brendan Hammond and Hilary Birtles. When can we go over?"

"Now if you like. The sea water will be a few inches deep in certain areas but it's safe to drive there. The sand is solid enough if you avoid the direct route."

"Weather wise?"

"It's cold yet it's holding, but we may get some showers later on. The big problem will be the wind. It can get fairly blowy out there."

"Doing what we can before the rain starts will be a good idea," said Brendan.

The Inspector acknowledged his colleague's suggestion and looked at Dawson. "And as far as you are aware no one is on the island, or at least should have been on the island?"

"No," replied the ranger, confidently. "No one's allowed to stay overnight."

The Inspector quickly interjected. "But if someone has…"

Dawson quickly interrupted. "I always do a final sweep either before it goes dark or when the tide dictates."

Even though she was not part of the discourse, Hilary interrupted the conversation. "Could someone simply hide?" The condescension in Hilary's voice put the ranger on the defensive.

"I don't check under every rock, there isn't time. In fact, I can't recall it ever happening before."

The Inspector gave Hilary a disapproving glance. He shivered and made sure the zip on his coat was as far up as it would go. "Shall we get a move on?"

Dawson rocked on his heels as the police officers began to move. "You can take your Range Rovers but your squad cars will never drive over the rocks."

"I thought you said it was sand," asked Watling.

"Once past the first Eye, you have to drive hard right and make your way across the rocks. There's only one way a vehicle can go but only those with a good clearance from the ground will make it."

Watling looked at his only suitable vehicle, which was the one he had just arrived in. The ambulance was paramount, but all the other cars were not designed for such an off road journey.

Commandeering the ranger's transport, he chose a team of nine including the two paramedics, Walker and Russell, the two forensic detectives, Brendan and Hilary and then there was Parker and himself. He ordered three uniformed officers, Clarke, Delaney and Morris to follow in Dawson's Range Rover.

Watling turned to leave but quickly turned back to Dawson. "What about keys?"

Dawson handed over a large bunch and then the keys to his Range Rover. "Each one is labelled. Do you need my help at all?"

"If a crime is suspected, no civilians I'm afraid." Watling then threw the car keys to Clarke and put the large bunch in his pocket. He felt he should have helped Hilary put her two cases into the back of his Range Rover but she was half his age and annoying so he slid into the passenger seat and waited for Parker to fire up the engine.

14:08pm

The sand was firm but ridged which, coupled with Parker's reckless speed, gave an uncomfortable ride for those travelling across it. The occupants of Watling's Range Rover were tossed from side to side with every dip and undulation. It was not strictly low tide so the vehicle sprayed its way through the puddles and streams that covered the barren expanse of sand, sending fountains of salt water across the windows. In the back seat, Brendan looked behind him through the drenched back windscreen and saw the blurred image of the small convoy trying to keep pace with them. He turned back when Watling spoke, his voice raised louder than normal to be heard over the din of the engine and the water cascading over the sides. "We can't go directly there, the sand is too soft." Watling drew his finger across the map sitting on his knee. "We have to drive around the Eyes."

"The Eyes?" remarked Hilary.

Watling pointed towards the distance. "The two smaller islands to the left are called the Little Eye and the Middle Eye."

Brendan leaned forward. "It sounds similar to a case my friend is investigating, well, she's more like a colleague, well, someone I know, well, more like a gob shite if you ask me." He leaned back. "What's actually on the island?" asked Brendan, as he felt the slight onset of motion sickness in his stomach.

Watling waited a second to see if Hilary was going to interrupt. He was not disappointed.

"According to a little bit of knowledge I possess," Hilary added, as if she was about to read it from a card she had prepared. "There are several buildings and outhouses. Some of them are privately owned, but the main cottages and houses are now abandoned."

"Does anyone live there?" asked Parker.

Hilary continued. "There was a permanent ranger presence until a couple of years ago. With no electric or running water on the island, I guess it's difficult to find anyone who wants to live there."

Brendan spoke again. "But they must have some sort of power."

"Gas bottles," replied Watling, in an effort for Hilary not to steal all of his thunder. "The ranger said there are a couple of gas fires and a cooker but that's your lot."

"Phone signal?" asked Hilary.

"There's a mast on the island. Why do you ask?"

"Jessica Puce who made the call said the only signal she could get was at Fog Cottage. But if there's a mast how could that have been the case?"

"If the mast was damaged?" said Watling. "Don't forget, we have that body the Coast Guard identified, so something's happened there."

14:10pm

With the speed of Parker's driving, it did not take long for the convoy to arrive at the Little Eye. He kept the glorified grassy knoll on his right turning almost ninety degrees once they had passed it. The Middle Eye loomed, its sandstone crag bore thousands of years of natural tidal damage and decay creating a jagged and ridged-like surface that blended with the sand around the base of the thirty foot cliffs. As they approached, Watling noticed a set of stone steps that led to the green, grassy peak. It was obvious the Middle Eye was devoid of any manmade structures and was just a pathway for walkers who did not want to traverse the slippery rocks around either side, a problem that Parker had finally slowed down for. There was a track, of sorts, but it was more of a route that was slightly flatter than any other possible way across the rocks. Watling thought about the word 'flat', although in his head this was an apt word considering the rocks either side of the track, however, the violent shaking of the car and its occupants, suggested otherwise. Watling held on tightly to the handle of the door and dashboard until his knuckles started to pale, but as soon as he felt his stomach start to twist they reached the short sandy beach area that ran around the southern edge of Hilbre Island.

Watling thought about the ambulance following behind them. He raised his radio to his lips. "Walker?"

The driver of the ambulance replied. *"Yes, Inspector."*

"How are you getting on?"

"A few scrapes to the undercarriage and it's a bit of a tight fit, width wise, but I think we'll get there without getting marooned."

"I'll leave you to concentrate on your driving." Watling lowered his radio and glanced in the wing mirror at the following vehicles slowly negotiating the hazardous terrain.

Parker stopped the Range Rover and pointed to the east and west side of the island. "We can't go any further except on to the island itself. The rocks are too jagged on either side."

"I can see why the coast guard couldn't get any closer," said Brendan, his face almost pressed against the door window. "Wait," Brendan leaned in between Watling and Parker and pointed to the cliff to their right. "There, can you see it?"

It took a couple of seconds for the passengers to acknowledge Brendan's discovery. Watling's eyes began to water as he stared, unblinking, at the body in the distance. It was not on the rocks as the coast guard had described, more stuck on something off the edge of the cliffs that surrounded the island. He finally blinked and turned to Parker. His voice was deep and gravelled in tone. "Get us on there."

Parker shifted the gear stick into first and drove over sandstone rock pools that had turned the sea water a rusty shade of red. He guided the vehicle around the western side and up a flat sandstone ramp that led to a single track road that had been cut into the rock. The drive to the summit was short, yet Watling found the scene to be quite breath-taking. It flattened out into a small green meadow. To their right was a small shack made of brick and slate and surrounded by wooden fencing. A little further along was a small white, stone cottage followed by another shack made of wood and slate, all bordered by a wooden panelled fence. The meadow soon sloped upwards into a large mound discoloured brown by decaying bracken and dying plants. It peaked with a rusted flag pole bearing a tattered green flag whose image had been lost in the years of being exposed to the unforgiving weather. It's dancing and flapping suggested the blustery breeze they had felt on the shore was a lot stronger now they were in the middle of the sea and Watling started to hope their time on the island would be quick while the elements were still being relatively kind to them.

The road continued along the west side of the island and any thoughts of their trip being any more than a tenuous lead in a suspected single homicide case were soon quelled when the body lying at the base of the mobile signal mast came into view. Parker slowed the Range Rover and eventually stopped several metres away. There was a stunned silence in the car. They were expecting to find one body, that of Jessica Puce, but a second meant something had happened over night on this remote, abandoned community and Watling started to fear for what else the island would reveal. "So much for the ranger's ban on overnight stays. I'll get the paramedics to take a look at it." He looked over his shoulder and saw the ambulance pull up behind them. He pressed the call button on his radio. "Walker, are you seeing this?"

The returning voice was clear. *"Yes, sir."*

"Looks like male. There seems to be a lot of blood as well."

"Russell and I will take a look."

"Thank you."

Brendan nodded to Hilary who opened the car door and slid out. Taking her case from the boot, she closed the car door and patted the roof.

"Parker, are you able to drive around it?" said Brendan, "we can't afford to contaminate the scene."

Parker nodded, and crept the car closer to the body. "There aren't any wires hanging from the box on the mast. Perhaps it isn't damaged."

Watling took his mobile phone from his pocket and looked at the full bars of signal on the device. He swapped back to his radio and spoke to Clarke, one of the uniforms in the commandeered ranger's vehicle bringing up the rear.

"Clarke, I need you to following me on to the island. We still need to reach the body on the east side. With the discovery of this second body, I think we should conduct a full search of the island."

"Yes, Boss."

Watling did not give a verbal order, instead, pointed towards the centre of the island and nodded. Parker acknowledged the gesture and carefully drove around the second body with the uniform officers just behind them mirroring his route. The road rose slightly until it reached a small white building to their right. Its glass front was curved one hundred and eighty degrees and was made up of several hundred small, square glass pieces, all framed in black.

"On the map this is the Telegraph Station," said Watling, but as soon as Parker drove the Range Rover around it, the rest of the island opened up in front of them. The collection of cottages, buildings and outhouses were back dropped in the distance by the vast empty space of sand and the gentle lapping of a dying tide. The West Kirby and Hoylake shoreline offered merely a thin break in the landscape between the pale sand and the dull, cloud filled sky. Parker stopped the vehicle and its occupants stretched their legs on the long, unkempt grass. Watling looked at his surroundings. The non-uniformity of the structures suggested they were buildings built for purpose yet nothing was ever knocked down. It was as if someone had lifted a large farm from the country side and placed it in the middle of the sea.

"It's weird don't you think?" said Brendan, as he picked up a handful of grass and let it float away in the wind.

"What is?" said Watling.

"If it wasn't for the taste of sea air you could believe we were on the Pennines."

Watling smirked. He looked to his left and saw a stone structure in the distance. "What's that?" he said, pointing and then looking at Parker.

Parker reached back into the Range Rover and took out the map. "The old lifeboat station. It just says 'un-used' on here."

Watling's radio crackled. It was Hilary. *"Male, late teens, early twenties. He's taken one hell of a beating."*

"A beating?"

"A heavy weapon looking at the trauma involved, fists possibly if the attacker was powerful enough."

"Ok, rope it off. We'll go and find the body on the east cliffs."

The Range Rover with the uniformed officers parked next to Watling, and he did not waste time in issuing Clarke and Delaney with orders. "Start searching every building, every crevice and behind every wall. Radio in if you find anything. The two of you can start with that lifeboat launch. Parker and Brendan, you go and find the body on the east cliffs. I'll join you in a minute." He looked at the remaining officer. He was young, inexperienced and new to his station. "What's your name again, son?"

"Morris, sir."

"Track back to those first three cottages. Do a sweep."

Morris nodded and walked back along the road. As everyone peeled away, Watling turned to investigate something he had noticed just before they had parked the vehicle. The curved window of the Telegraph Station rankled his intuition to the point where he stepped closer to the building. Its dark interior initially prevented him from identifying the long, dark smear across the inside of the glass, but as he slowly approached, he felt his stomach begin to knot. The congealed red streak of blood was spattered from the bottom to the top of the window. He sighed, closed his eyes and pushed his hands into his pockets because through the dried crimson stain he could make out the figure of another body lying face down on the floor. "Jesus Christ, what happened here?" He walked around the back of the building and was about to try the weather-worn door, when his radio sparked into life.

"Delaney here, Boss."

Watling raised the radio to his lips. "Go ahead."

"Sir, we have another body, possibly male."

"In the lifeboat station?"

"Negative, Boss. On the rocks along the western side of the island."

"Cause of death?"

"Unknown, we're looking for a way down."

"Ok, preserve the scene once you're there." Watling lowered the radio and thought for a couple of seconds before raising it back up to his mouth. He was about to speak when Parker's voice interrupted him.

"Excuse me, Boss?"

"What is it, Parker?"

"I think you should see this."

14:27pm

Watling walked down the grassed area and on to the driveway that led into the heart of the buildings. He passed a well-kept, green painted shack, an open garage containing a trailer, and the small ranger station before pushing open a large wooden gate as if he was gaining entrance to an abandoned farmyard. Building materials, rope, planks of wood, pieces of broken safety barrier and bags of hardened cement littered the small crevices the haphazard layout of the buildings allowed, in an attempt to 'put them out of the way somewhere' but with little success.

As he made his way to the eastern cliffs, he passed a small, thin, whitewashed cottage on his right. Its dirty, grime-ridden walls ended with a small, black door, its wooden panels flaking and damaged through severe weather and lack of maintenance. A grey, wooden name plate was held to the door by two rusted nails that were not flush to the wood, suggesting little care was taken in its fixing. It displayed two words at a slight angle as if the lettering was written in a hurry. The words were, 'Fog Cottage'. Watling felt a chill when he saw a broken padlock lying on the floor, and, with his foot, he gently pushed open the door.

There was an unpleasant smell in the thin cottage, and it was obvious the one room was used more for storage as the only furniture it contained was piled against each other and resided with more wooden panels and broken safety barriers. The cottage was dark, the ceiling was low and Watling felt himself short of breath as the damp atmosphere clambered into his lungs. He took out his phone, raised an eyebrow at the full signal and was about to place it back into his jacket when the smear of blood on the floor caught his eye. He crouched, looking for any other evidence, and when the widespread spray of blood across the lower part of the right hand wall came into his view, he stepped backwards and out of the cottage so as to prevent any further contamination.

He turned quickly when he heard Parker call his name. When he approached, he offered Watling a plastic bag containing a mobile phone. Watling took it; it still had a little power.

Parker pointed to the part of the screen where the Inspector should press but when Watling tried the suggestion it was unresponsive. "The screen doesn't work through the plastic, Inspector, but according to the log, the last call was to Aaron Childs and I don't think you'll be surprised to find that Aaron Childs is also the first name in the contact list. My guess is that this is not Jessica Puce's phone and she called Aaron for help because his name was first on the list."

"Why not call the Police?" Watling felt a little frustrated. "How difficult is it to dial three nines?"

Parker continued. "As soon as she made the call, she took a blow to the head and then dragged herself down this path. You can follow the blood trail." He pointed at the red marks that soiled the stony ground.

Watling crouched once more and looked closer at the droplets of blood. "Dragged herself along or was dragged along?"

Parker agreed. "It's difficult to tell".

Watling stood up when Parker turned to move away. He followed the Sergeant, all the time careful not to stand on any evidence, and they walked between two buildings and down a short, narrow path that led to a set of well worn, uneven stone steps covered in dead and dying bracken. The staircase was cut into the eastern side of the island, its raised sides were over-grown with weeds and it turned slightly to the right the further it reached to the water's edge. A treacherous walk in the dark and the rain, thought Watling as he placed his first boot on the top step. It was a way to access the sea, obviously, for visiting boats when the tide was fully in, which is why a corroded, misshapen, wire frame gate was hinged into the left-hand cliff side. It was here Jessica Puce's body was swinging. Her right leg was lodged inside the gate's frame along with her right wrist which was twisted back on itself giving her elbow a disjointed look. Her body hung from the rusted gate and over the last of the steps causing her corpse to gently sway to the accompaniment of the whine and squeal of the grinding metal when the wind swirled through the gap.

Brendan was crouched next to Jessica's body but stood up and walked up the steps as soon as he saw Watling. "I've not touched anything yet, but I think it's obvious she fell down these steps at speed. There are wounds to her cranium, right arm and right cheek."

"Another beating?" said Watling, walking past the forensic pathologist.

"It looks that way."

Watling crouched next to the body. Jessica's eyes were open which gave her a lifeless stare through the thin strands of wet hair covering half of her face. Her right cheek was indeed cut, with circled bruising around it and it was mottled with dried blood and dirt. "And we know this is Jessica Puce, how?"

Parker walked down the steps and gave his tablet containing Jessica's profile and statistics to Watling. "It's just come through from Chatham at HQ."

Watling took the tablet, looked at the image and then back at the body hanging from the iron gate. A thread of sadness spun around his heart and he shook his head as he tossed the tablet back to Parker who juggled it under control. "We can't leave her like this. Get her down Brendan, as quick as you can."

Brendan nodded to Watling as the Inspector took his phone from his pocket. "We're going to need some help. I don't think the weather is going to be on our side."

"Help?" protested Brendan. "Hilary and I…"

Watling interrupted. "We have a body in the Telegraph Station and one on the rocks near the lifeboat station. We don't have a lot of time."

14:53pm

Watling finished the last of his phone calls, took the keys from his pocket and sorted out the silver yale with the 'Ranger Cabin' label dangling from its steel ring. He threw it to Parker and instructed him to set up the incident room just as Officer Morris was walking towards them from the parked cars.

"Anything, Morris?"

"Nothing, Boss."

Watling gave a slight gesture with his head and Morris followed him further into the heart of the island. The complex of buildings was dog legged in nature with two access points to their rear, either by following the narrow alleyway that ran like a ginnel behind the back of the structures or along the raised over- grown heath that sloped upwards until it overlooked the track on the western side of the island they initially drove along. They walked between a white washed pseudo cottage and an approximately five foot sandstone wall, the top of it being the start of the small patch of grass land, as if the alley had been cut into the large grassy knoll. The wall of the building was also sandstone, the blocks beaten by the weather, displaying pock marks in the golden brown patches where the paint had peeled and fallen away. Grit and dust that had fallen from the walls crunched underneath their feet as they followed the ginnel's sharp left and then right. There was a shed to their left and Watling rattled the padlock on its door until Morris noticed the back entrance of the next building was ajar. The dull, grey, crumbling plaster mirrored the dark clouds appearing overhead, threatening to make Watling's investigation a logistical headache, but help was on its way, however, and they could not come quick enough, he thought, as he pushed open the door a little further.

The house was large and derelict. The taste of dust and stale air quickly found their way to the back of his throat and he cleared it several times which accompanied the echoes of his heavy steps on the wooden floor. The house was plain and without decoration or ornaments hanging from the wall, as if it had been stripped bare ready for demolition. Only the rusted cooker and cracked porcelain sink suggested the room to his left had once been a kitchen. There were four other large rooms downstairs, each with their floorboards exposed, their fireplaces removed and their walls cracked and peeling. The echo of Morris's trudge up the staircase seemed to shudder the whole house. His pacing across the upstairs rooms and landing felt to Watling like the ceilings were going to give way as plumes of grit floated down from the cracks. When Morris appeared at the top of the stairs, he shrugged his shoulders.

"Nothing?" asked Watling.

Morris began to walk down the stairs. "Empty and cold, colder than down here at least. It gave me the shivers, prickling the skin, in fact."

Watling walked back out of the house and further along the alleyway. Morris followed, and they dog-legged to the right. The next building was also like a glorified terrace house but it was obvious it had been built at a different time from the one they had just vacated. The smooth cut sandstone had once been whitewashed but there was very little of the white left. It existed in cracks and fractures giving outlines to the large and un-uniform nature of the blocks. He peered through its grime streaked windows and noticed furniture. A couch, an armchair, a small chest acting as a coffee table and a sideboard gave indications of life, but it did not look maintained. Homely, certainly, but more of an escape from the bitter cold, a refuge to those who worked on the island or those who were stranded. The next window along revealed a double bed. It was made but it was the only piece of furniture in the room, indicating once again the house was more of a functioning facility than any type of actual 'home'.

There certainly weren't any signs of a struggle, at least nothing the view from the windows would allow. The back door, however, had been forced open. It was still locked; however, the part of the lock that should reside in the frame of the door was on the ground, ripped away from the damp, rotten wood.

"Easy access," he said, drawing his finger along what remained of the lock. But as he slowly pushed open the back door, he knew something was wrong. The pungent smell of iron filings was too familiar to Watling. It was the aroma of dripping blood and open wounds. Before entering the kitchen, he reassured Morris, who was screwing his face up at the sickening atmosphere. On the table were several supermarket bags containing uncooked meats, biscuits and alcohol. "Overnight stay," he said, looking at the cheap, non-patterned plates that sat on the shelves. He stood still, his eyes checking every corner of the room, only stopping when he saw the blood spatter on the floor by the half open door in the opposite wall. He sighed, let his head drop and it was almost with a heavy heart that Watling began to follow the trail. His macabre sense of trepidation was justified as he saw two bodies lying in the middle of the long thin room, their limbs contorted, bent into positions only a break to the bone would grant. There were open gashes to their faces and heads, the power of the blows were suggested by the red spray spread wide across the dirty white walls and dusty furniture. Morris stood still while Watling kneeled next to the bodies. Able to keep his disgust hidden within his gut, Watling looked at both bodies from several angles.

"Male and female, young, possibly the same age as the others."

Morris shifted uncomfortably. "What are your thoughts, Boss?"

"They've both taken quite a beating which is consistent with the other victims, but my guess is they'd all planned an illegal stay over and either one of them did this or there was someone on this island they weren't expecting." Watling eyed a bloodied, sharp edged rock under an armchair and could only imagine the horrific beating the two victims had received. Their mutilated limbs, their cracked skulls and crimson covered, broken faces suggested severe rage, anger beyond all reason. Watling knew such crimes were usually unplanned and the perpetrators easy to catch, but this did not make him feel any less sickened. Yet, there was something he was missing. He stood up and looked out of the front window at a small patio area.

"You saw nothing in your sweep, Morris?"

"No sir."

Watling thought for a moment. "The tide's been out all morning, and we're the first people on the island."

"I guess so."

"And we didn't see anyone leaving as we arrived."

A realisation came over Morris' face before it turned to expression of worry. He looked at Watling who was staring back at him, holding his finger over his lips.

The faint shuffle above them meant there was somebody upstairs.

15:12pm

The threadbare carpet on the stairs muffled Watling's and Morris's ascent but it did not completely disguise their movements. Watling listened carefully to the continuous shuffling. Whoever it was knew little of their presence or perhaps just did not care they were in the house. They reached the landing but

Morris's clumsy boot on an unsecured floorboard caused the panel to raise and drop back into place. The shuffling stopped. Watling, realising their stealthy approach had failed, took the radio from his belt. "Parker, update please."

"Entering the house now."

"Make sure no-one comes down the stairs."

Watling put back his radio. There was only one room with a closed door and, when the shuffling began again, it was obvious there was someone beyond the threshold. He nodded to Morris who swallowed hard. Taking the handle in his shaking hand, Watling counted down from three before forcing open the door and rushing inside with Morris following. What they found was a single bed, a wardrobe and a wicker chair. Watling stood puzzled for a moment before checking the contents of the wardrobe, which, like the room, was empty. Morris looked underneath the bed while Watling inspected the latches of the closed window but they soon turned to each other and shrugged their shoulders. Watling felt almost foolish as he stood, hands on hips in the empty room. He felt his eyes strain and then his vision blur slightly so he rubbed them with his fingers. His spine shivered and his skin prickled as he felt the coolness that seemed to follow Parker up the stairs.

"It's a mess down there," said Parker, as he checked all of the upstairs with Morris.

"I want a register of who arrives and leaves this island," Watling insisted. "Whoever did this, unless he or she swam to shore or used a boat, could very well be still on the island, hiding certainly, but still here." He took the phone from his pocket. "We need more manpower."

15:38pm

The familiar smell of blood stirred the bile in Watling's stomach as he walked into the Telegraph Station. Hilary was kneeling down, performing a visual inspection of the gnarled body. She acknowledged his presence with a simple nod and carried on looking at the battered corpse. Yet when Watling was about to move, she spoke without looking his way. "I got over here as fast as I could."

Watling went to move.

Hilary barked back at him. "Mind where you put your feet."

"Why?"

"I've only had the chance to do a visual inspection. I've still not finished with the victim by the phone mast." She gestured at Watling to move closer to the exit. "We're going to need more than Brendan and myself otherwise we're going to be here all night."

Watling took a few steps towards the door. "It's in hand."

"I think it's probable to say this girl staggered through the door, fell in the middle of the room and managed to crawl a couple of feet towards the window."

Watling looked at the crimson smears on dark brown stained floorboards. "The girl?"

"Late teens, early twenties."

"Like the others, then."

"Multiple traumas to her face including the frontal bone, mandible, glabella and occipital bone. I also think her clavicle is broken along with a few ribs and the shaft of humerus in both arms…"

"Jesus," said Watling, interrupting.

Hilary continued. "The tibia and the patella as well."

"Patella?"

"The right knee is not at its natural angle. I would suggest the kneecap had been knocked out of place."

"With what?"

"A heavy club or an iron bar. But what I can't understand is why the whole body?"

"I don't understand."

"Break the knees to stop your victim from running away, that I can follow, but it's not just the knees and head, it's all over, the ankle, hip, shin. The victim near the telephone mast was the same. It seems…" Hilary paused, thinking for an appropriate word until Watling chose one for her.

"Frenzied."

Hilary turned back to the body. "It's vicious. The trauma around the head suggests this girl should have died after a couple of blows, but I don't think the killer stopped even after her death."

Specks of blood blurred the text of the small historical account of the island hanging from the wood panelling, and the spray pattern of red that stained the white ceiling proved that whoever she was had the life hammered from her. The concentration of spatter was across the concave window, the feature which had drawn Watling's attention from the exterior of the building.

Hilary rocked back on her haunches. "Has a murder weapon been found?"

Watling scoffed. "In one of the other buildings. A rock, under an arm chair."

"That's odd, why leave the murder weapon there. It's literally a stone's throw to the sea; why not chuck it in there? Was this rock jagged in any way?"

"A little, why?"

"These wounds were made by a more blunt object."

Officer Morris appeared at the door. "Inspector."

Watling turned, "Are they here?"

"Yes, sir."

15:49pm

"Inspector Watling, quite the mess you have."

The hand shake was strong and firm. Watling smirked slightly, "Inspector Cosgrove, I'm so glad you could make it, we need you urgently."

Cosgrove held the handshake. "Really? What for?"

"We need the bins emptying in the Ranger Station."

Cosgrove laughed and proceeded with a more informal greeting. "George."

"Merv," said Watling, finally breaking from the handshake.

"Have you called anyone else?"

"Murphy from Merseyside."

"Oh Christ, it must be one hell of a mess if you've invited him."

"He's good, has the resources and the weather's going to ruin our day if we don't get a move on."

"The Ogress might accompany him, though."

"I wouldn't have thought so, she never leaves her den."

Cosgrove looked about him. "This is not a place I would expect a crime scene."

Watling nodded. "It certainly wasn't what I was expecting when I woke up this morning. Your people are coming?"

"They'll be here within five minutes. They're going to have fun and games negotiating that rocky track. So then George, what do we have?"

Watling cleared his throat. "So far, one male, late teens or early twenties, at the telephone mast on the way in…"

Cosgrove interrupted. "Yeah, I saw that one. Nasty."

"Another male on the rocks near the lifeboat station. I have Brendan on that one at the moment because we've got to get him moved before the tide comes in."

"What else?"

"A female in the Telegraph Station, we're not sure but it looks like she was first beaten outside, staggered inside the station and then beaten some more. We also have another female, the erstwhile Miss Jessica Puce, caught in the frame of the gate that leads down to the east side rocks, and lastly we have a male and female in the sandstone house in the cluster of buildings further inland. All of them, like the first victim, in their late teens or early twenties."

"Six? You only had four when the call came."

"And another thing, if the killer didn't get away by boat or drown in the sea, then he or she could very well still be here."

Cosgrove stared at Watling. "You need help with the search?"

"I'd like your forensics on the two bodies in the house. Hilary will take a look after your lot have finished."

Cosgrove interrupted. "I have Maduka and Bretton at my disposal."

"Excellent, we're going to need lights, power, provisions and yes, your help with the search would be much appreciated. No-one should be alone. We need to double up on every post just in case our chap, or chapette, didn't leave."

"Anything else?"

"Once the tide rolls in and we lose the daylight, we're on our own. We need the names of everyone who is willing to stay over and get the job done."

"What numbers are you thinking of?"

"Between forensics, paramedics, us and uniform, I would say four or five per victim."

"You do know Murphy's going to want his forensics to look at each body as well."

"I expect nothing less; we've got to keep the lawyers happy, eh?"

Cosgrove sniggered and spoke into his radio. "Hawkins, are you there?"

"Yes, sir."

"How far are you out?"

"Thirty seconds, if that, this track is a bit of a tight squeeze."

"We're going to have to work quickly, and get extra uniform here, we need to search the entire island."

Watling looked at his watch, 15:54. They would be lucky if they had ninety minutes of daylight left.

16:09pm

Watling stepped carefully across the jagged, sandstone rocks towards the back of the island until he reached the lifeboat station. The building was an empty shell, unused in decades. It was made from large square blocks of cut sandstone and plaster which had been battered and worn down, like the rest of the structures, through years of the unforgiving elements. A green door was home to a life saver ring, however, another doorway just to its right led into the heart of the station. The relatively small building was more of a slow ramp surrounded by thick walls to protect the lifeboat that was once stationed there. It was now but an echo of its former life. The track like grooves in the stone and the vertical structures jutting out of the walls gave an insight into the building's previous activities, but the slime and algae covered ramp that stretched far into the sea, told Watling that, like the island itself, the human need for it was behind them and everything they had built on this tiny green meadow was now left to ruin.

He left the lifeboat station and made his way left along the cliff edge, all the time watching where he was putting his feet as he felt the wind begin to swirl around him. After only a few metres he finally saw Brendan and Officer Clarke, some twelve feet below him, busying themselves around a body that lay contorted on the rocks. He caught Brendan's attention who beckoned him down. The wind was strong enough to render anything being shouted at him as just fragments of sound and when Watling shrugged his shoulders at him, Brendan eventually pointed at the side of the cliff just to Watling's left.

Looking over the edge, Watling could see a strip of iron built into the cliff face. Semi circles of two differing sizes were cut into the metal at regular points, perfect footholds and handholds as he began to ease himself over the edge. The iron ladder was old and rusty but it was well made and easily held his weight, however, it did not stop him jumping off to the rocks when he was only three quarters of the way down.

"I'm too old for this sort of thing," he said, gathering himself.

Brendan looked over to him. "It's not what you expect to see in the side of an island. A smugglers ladder perhaps."

"It's got to be easier going up it," replied Watling. "It can't be a coincidence there's one of our victims here."

Brendan stood up and stretched his back. "My early assumptions were that this body was washed up as I'm sure the water comes up to this point when the tide is in, but he certainly didn't drown."

Watling looked down at the contorted body. "Jesus, is his…"

"Neck broken, yes." Brendan kneeled down, took a pencil from his pocket and pointed at certain points of the body. "The right elbow is broken, there is bruising to the back of the head, the nose is broken, there is bruising on both cheeks and around the midriff and there are several teeth missing."

"Could he have fallen?"

"Yes, but these injuries were not made from any fall. That iron ladder is twelve, fourteen feet at the most. He was either beaten at the top of the cliff and thrown down, or thrown down and then beaten. Looking at the amount of bruising, I would entertain both explanations."

"Beaten with what?"

"Any sort of blunt object, fists perhaps, certainly nothing sharp."

"Hilary's victim, the one near the phone mast, was badly beaten as well, and Jessica Puce was in a similar state. Could this person have been trying to escape or at least hide?"

"It's possible. The ladder is the safest way down to the rocks, although, as a hiding place, I'm sure there are more creative and less dangerous ones."

"But, it is highly possible that he was running from someone, hence why he's down here and the rest of the bodies are in and around the buildings."

"Agreed," said Brendan. "For the record, his name is Harry Alter."

"How d'you know that?"

"I've just finished bagging up the contents of his pockets." Brendan picked up the evidence bags and held them out for the Inspector. "Lighter, papers and a small bag of weed, forty two pence in loose change and his wallet with sixty quid in notes."

"Not a robbery then."

"The beating is savage; one could argue that it's almost frenzied. Any criminal psychologist would say the attack, and probably the others, were not motivated by money."

Watling remained silent for a few seconds before clearing his throat . "Any sign of a weapon?"

"Brendan and I have looked but not found one so far, Inspector," said Clarke, before answering the call on his radio. "Yes, he's here, I'll tell him."

Watling looked at Clarke. "Inspector Murphy's finally arrived I would guess."

Clarke nodded. "Yes Boss and he's not alone."

Watling looked towards the sky. "Oh shit, so she has ventured out from her stink pit."

"You'll be the first one to test the ladder going up," quipped Brendan. "Don't forget, we need the paramedics as soon as you can. We're exposed to the elements out here."

Watling turned and cautiously, started to climb up the iron ladder.

16:17pm

Watling met up with Inspector Murphy outside the Telegraph Station. After shaking his hand, Watling noticed on the other side of the curved window, two forensic officers attending to the body. "I didn't authorise this," said Watling to Murphy. "I'm lead on this investigation."

"Not anymore." The reply was not that of Murphy's. All Murphy could do was smirk and look to his right. Ever since Clarke had mentioned Inspector Murphy was not alone, Watling had suspected such a takeover was going to be forthcoming. Chief Inspector Eleanor Bright took off the leather glove from her right hand by tugging at each individual finger. She held out her exposed hand for Watling to take."

"Watling, good to see you. I've heard good things," said the Chief Inspector, with an overly booming, masculine tone, and she imposed her authority by crushing the hand of her inferior.

Watling knew she was lying, it wasn't good for her to see him, she doesn't like meeting anyone, or at least that is what he had heard, but he played along. "Likewise, Ma'am, it's good to have you with us, we could do with all the help we can get." He was almost glad when she released the vice-like grip she had on his knuckles.

"It might be bracing, but I couldn't miss this one, it's all very mysterious don't you think?"

"Ma'am."

"And besides, a good and efficient clean-up operation means a happy police force, happy tax payers and happy victims' families."

"I don't think the victims' families…"

"They'll be happy in the knowledge that the region's finest are doing their upmost to catch their son's or daughter's killer, agreed?"

"I guess so," said Watling. "But I would like to point out that this is my investigation, yet someone has put forensics to work on the victim in the Telegraph Station."

"I had officers standing idle and I'd heard the Inspector in charge was off catching crabs in a rock pool somewhere, so I set them to work. So, Watling, where are we up to?"

"Six victims, early reports suggest they were all beaten. I have opted for a team of four for each body and, with the weather getting worse and the chance of rain quite likely, I thought of getting them picked up by helicopter."

"No, no, no, Inspector. The wind is too strong for helicopters. With the tide coming in, we'll have to bag them up and get them picked up by ambulance when the tide is back out. Here's what's going to happen; we have six forensics, one for each victim. The Paramedics already here can stay and assist. The rest of uniform will do a fine toothed comb of the island. Once done, we'll break into teams to either help forensics or settle us in for a cold night."

"You're staying until the tide goes back out?" asked Watling, slightly surprised.

"This'll be a high profile case, it looks better if I'm over-seeing the proceedings." A gust of wind caused Eleanor to hold onto her hat. "Inspector Murphy, you head back to Hoylake, chummy up the media and make sure no-one comes anywhere near this island."

"Yes, Ma'am ."

As Murphy turned to leave the island, Eleanor walked towards the Ranger Station. "Watling, with me, and get Cosgrove on the radio, we need an incident room and teams to search the Island."

Watling protested. "But I've got all of that in hand."

"Quickly, Inspector," was the blunt reply he received.

17:15pm

As the grim November evening began to encompass the sky, the halogen glow from each crime scene gave the island a spectral luminosity, an eerie backdrop that was in similar keeping to the macabre work being carried out. Lamps were also set up at certain points along paths to allow the safe passage from scene to scene. Eleanor Bright upturned her collar as light rain swirled in the heavy wind and against her face. She swore to herself because she was thinking why on earth didn't she delegate this overseeing malarkey to Murphy? It was then she recalled the reason why. The administration error yet to come to light to which an efficient operation on Hilbre Island may, or may not, there wasn't any guarantee at this moment, act as a smokescreen, or at least deflect some of the potential outrage. She walked along the main drive and approached Hilary who was still working on the victim lying next to the telephone mast. Before she made her presence known, she neatened up her collar and walked as if the bad weather was not affecting her. "Have you had a break, Hilary?"

Hilary looked up. She was a little taken back by the Chief Inspector's approach. She stood up, took her rubber gloves off and re-tied her hair into a smarter looking ponytail. "I haven't had a chance."

"Have you nearly finished?"

"Almost, half an hour, maybe more, maybe less."

"Just in time with the rain finally coming. Are you ok, Hilary?"

"Apologies, Ma'am, but I didn't think you knew who I was."

Eleanor snorted and put her hands behind her back. "It is my job to know who people are, even if they aren't under my command. Word travels fast if someone is making a good impression and I hear a lot about you."

Slightly embarrassed, Hilary cleared her throat and tried to act modest. "I'm just trying to do a good job."

"Are you happy working for Brendan?"

"He's taught me a lot. Apparently he's retiring soon and I'm his contingency plan."

Eleanor clicked her tongue. "Brendan's contingency plan, I don't know how you coped with the flattery."

"He's been good to me, but I don't think Inspector Watling wants him to retire, so I get the cold shoulder a lot of the time."

"Have you ever thought about working for Liverpool?"

"It's crossed my mind, yes."

"Excellent." Eleanor smiled and put up the collar on her coat. "Once this is over, we should have a chat about your prospects."

Hilary felt a few butterflies in her stomach. "I would like that very much."

"Mum's the word though for the time being." Eleanor put a finger across her lips.

Hilary nodded.

"Thirty minutes you said."

"Possibly, less this chat of course."

Eleanor looked at the body. "Regardless, I want everyone in the incident room by 17:45 for a situation report."

Hilary turned and continued her work. As Eleanor walked slowly away, she held her radio to her lips. "This is Chief Inspector Bright..." she held the radio away from her when loud static came from the speaker. It took a couple of seconds for it to subside but then an undercurrent of crackles continued when she repeated her opening statement. "This is Chief Inspector Bright, situation report in the incident room at 17:45, all to attend, please."

17:45pm

Watling was the last to arrive at the Ranger Station and struggled to find an empty space to stand. The Station was more of a glorified port-a-cabin furnished with a couple of tables, filing cabinets, a desk and a set of drawers. It certainly wasn't meant to comfortably house twenty six people, which of course it didn't, not comfortably at least. However, twenty six people were making the best of their own small space, whether it was leaning against a wall, perched on the edge of a table or the luxury of actually sitting in a cheap, plastic chair. Even with the weight of the congested conditions, the Ranger Station seemed to move and rattle in the increasingly strong winds. Without power on the island, a halogen lamp was set up just inside the door. It pointed to the ceiling, and, although it illuminated the desperate lick of paint the Ranger Station needed, it also reflected the light on its grey surface and lit up the room with a soft, white radiance. It was, without question, light enough for Eleanor to see her audience fidgeting, which is why she quickly asked for quiet.

"Now that we're all here." Eleanor looked at Watling. There began a murmur as all the room's occupants began to talk to one another until Eleanor thumped her fist onto the desk. The instant silence was followed by a soft, 'thank you', from Eleanor's lips.

"When you have all quite finished." Eleanor turned to the white board behind her and picked up the blue dry marker and dirty blue cloth sitting on the shelf next to her. After rigorously removing the previous scribble and notes, she flipped the top from the marker and began to write as she spoke.

"As you probably don't know each other, except for those associated with you own station, we have teams from three different forces. Liverpool, led by myself, Wirral, led by Inspector Watling and North Wales, led by Inspector Cosgrove. Each team consists of eight members and is a mix of forensics, uniform and paramedics. It was Inspector Watling's recommendation there should be four personnel per victim, hence all of your good selves. As you are aware, we are on an island. In forty-five minutes the tide will be fully in. Once it is then we'll be cut off for about nine hours, which means the earliest we can all go home is around three-thirty in the morning." Eleanor paused to let the news sink in. She expected at least some muttering but there was only the sound of the wind rattling the frame of the Station. "If any of you don't wish to spend the night on the island, speak now as this is your last chance to leave."

Seconds passed but no one neither spoke nor raised their arm. Eleanor felt a proud glow inside her belly and continued.

"There's food in one of the houses as well as a gas powered urn, so hot drinks are plentiful. It's going to be a cold night so you all need to be fed and watered. I will need two from uniform to organise this straight after this briefing."

She looked at the members of her team. "Constable Walsh? Can you see to this, as well as…?" Eleanor looked at Kevin Walsh as he nodded his agreement. She looked at the rest of the faces and pointed at one she did not recognise. "Constable, what's your name?"

"Alston, Ma'am."

"Can you help Walsh with this?"

Alston nodded and then acknowledged Walsh who was looking at her.

"There will not be any helicopter support due to the high winds, likewise with boats, so the extraction of our victims will not be done until tomorrow morning. Let's make sure they're bagged up and ready to go for before then. This leads me on to the victims themselves. Inspector Watling?"

Eleanor stood aside and Watling shuffled his way to the white board. He smoothed down his jacket and seemed slightly nervous, as if he found speaking in front of a group of people quite challenging. Knowing there was a room full of eyes waiting for him to start he stammered his opening line.

"I've a feeling we're not all here. I only counted twenty-six when there should be twenty-seven of us." There was a soft murmur in the room as its occupants looked about each other, but stopped when Inspector Cosgrove spoke.

"It's Aaralyn."

"Who?" replied Eleanor.

"Officer Aaralyn Skanthavarathan, she's one of mine."

The Chief Inspector had trouble regurgitating the name. "Skanthava…what?"

"Skanthavarathan," said Cosgrove, correcting his superior. "She must still be outside."

Eleanor scoffed. "She's obviously looking for more letter 'A's for her name." The quip caused the room to fall silent. She swallowed hard in the awkward silence and gestured for Watling to carry on.

"Who was the last to see her?" The faces in the room were nonplussed and he only waited a few seconds before continuing. "You were meant to be working in pairs. Why wasn't she with someone?" There was more silence. "What was she working on?"

"She was searching the island," said Officer London, "but that was before it went dark."

Watling looked at Cosgrove. "Inspector, can you try and get her on the radio?"

"The radios are playing up a bit."

"Try a quick scout around instead, while I carry on with the brief? The weather is getting worse and only the main paths are lit."

Cosgrove nodded. He turned up the collar on his jacket and everyone felt the wind swirl around them as Cosgrove opened the door and left the Ranger Station.

Watling cleared his throat and consulted the notes he had made.

"We have six victims all aged between eighteen and twenty-one. Jessica Puce, Harry Alter, Graham Spence, Marian Pendlebury, Kara Winston and Toby Brashear. We know because their personal effects were still on their person, suggesting this, along with the remote location, was not multiple homicides due to robbery. Jessica Puce was twisted in the gates that lead down to the water on the eastern side of the island. Graham Spence is the victim we all met next to the phone mast on our way here. Harry Alter is the body on the rocks near the old lifeboat station. Marian Pendlebury is the victim in the Telegraph Station, which leaves Kara Winston and Toby Brashear as the remaining bodies located in one of the main buildings. The cause of death seems to be the same for all six victims and that is multiple blunt force traumas about the body from the legs to the head. I think, 'frenzied', is the word continuously being used by our forensics team and, from what I've seen, I see no reason at this stage to disagree with them. Motivation, at present, is unknown. However, with robbery taken out of the equation, another motive could be revenge. It could very well be that one of them murdered the other five but this doesn't explain how they themselves took such a beating. If it was done by people or persons unknown then they are hiding, escaped in a boat of some description or attempted to swim back to the mainland. It can be surmised that our six victims were either staying over on the island for a bet or a dare. If some lunatic wanted to kill them then this would be a perfect opportunity to do it. Forensics team, once you have completed your analysis on your assigned victim, please speak to Brendan who will delegate you to one of the other bodies. I don't want anything to be missed but bear in mind haste, the less contamination from the elements the better." Watling looked at Brendan. "Let's get Graham Spence, the victim near the iron ladder, sorted and moved first."

Brendan nodded his agreement.

"We've gone over every inch of this island, so I want all available units to check for evidence in the buildings. Bag anything you think maybe important. If forensics requires your help, give it. Let's keep busy, let's keep warm. It's going to be a long evening." Watling drew out the last syllable of the word 'evening' when he heard a grating sound along the outer wall of the Ranger Station. The others had heard it too and they began to murmur between themselves as their gaze followed the scraping as it moved along the side of the building. The noise stopped when it reached the window. Watling quickly drew a torch from his pocket, twisted the end until the beam shone at the ceiling and then pointed it at the glass. Even through the glare from the reflection of the light, Watling could not see anyone outside. The murmuring in the room started again but Watling waved his arm up and down and turned to the others with his finger on his lips. The hushed room quickly unveiled the grating sound once more. Watling followed its path with his torch as it continued underneath the window.

"Who is it?" asked Officer Staines.

Watling took the radio from his pocket, but pressing the button emitted a burst of static and then a constant crackle of white noise. He held it to his mouth and increased the volume of his voice to break through the seemingly fractured radio waves.

"Inspector Cosgrove, can you hear me?" Watling waited for a response but it was as if the radio was broken.

Eleanor Bright tried her own radio but received the same white noise. "What's going on?"

Watling rushed to the door and grabbed the handle. The scraping had stopped but Watling hurried out of the hut and around the right hand side of the building. He was met by the officers who had run left, but there was no one to be seen. Watling drew his fingers across the side of the hut before ushering the others back into the Ranger Station. He tried the radio once more but received the same fizz of static. The wind threw rain into his face and, for a brief moment, he stood with his eyes closed. It felt like the elements were cleansing him of his anxieties as his rational thoughts surmised that the flimsy structure of the Ranger Station would simply exaggerate a stick or a piece of left over building debris, of which there was a lot scattered about, should it clatter into the building in such a strong wind. However, the broken radio was odd, he thought to himself, as he made his way back.

Once in the room, Watling did not bother to settle everyone down, instead he just spoke loudly enough to be heard over the chattering officers. "Excitement over, ok everyone, you know what to do. Let's get on with it."

The Ranger Station emptied within seconds leaving only Watling and Eleanor in the glow of the halogen lamp. Watling looked at the Chief Inspector. "Anything you need me to do?"

Eleanor stared back, "Just carry on, Inspector."

Watling opened the door and was about to leave the building when he stopped and turned. "Off the record…" he closed the door, "…and between you and me, of course."

"Of course."

"Why are you really here?"

"P.R. We've got to be seen to be proactive, resourceful, it's all about getting results. This is going to be a high profile case."

Watling folded his arms. "And this has nothing to do with Operation Jackdaw?"

"How did you know about that? Was it Murphy?"

"Honestly, between you and I?"

"Okay, maybe, just a little. I'm not going to let that balls-up tarnish my tenure in this position."

"Do you think a 'by the books' operation on this Island is going to deflect the media away from the death of a kid in one of your cells?"

"You're out of line, Watling."

Watling unfolded his arms in the awkward silence that followed and then stepped out of the station and into the swirling winds.

18:25pm

The smell of death still lingered in the building, Watling had remembered it well when he and Morris first entered it. The two bodies still lay in the same position and the floor was still stained with crimson, but this time the room was well lit which accentuated the dust and decay in its seventies design. The corpses were at the attention of Hilary and the Paramedics, Walker and Russell. Hilary was crouched over the female body and did not lift her head when Watling spoke her name. Either she did not hear him or chose to ignore his presence; he suspected the latter so he spoke again. "Are you nearly finished?"

Without looking up, Hilary sighed and made it look like an effort to get to her feet as if his being in the room was putting her out. "I've only just started and I'd get this one done a lot quicker without interruptions."

"Good because we don't have a lot of time."

Hilary placed the heel of her left palm against her forehead. "Tell that to the Ogress. She seems more interested in offering me a job than sorting this mess out."

Watling could not help feeling a slight pang of exhilaration at the thought of Hilary leaving his station. "It could be a good career move. Liverpool's a bigger pond."

"True, but I'm not sure trying to answer questions about my career whilst I've got my hands on a cadaver is the best time to make any sort of decision like that."

As quick as the pang had come, it was gone and Watling, after finally obtaining Hilary's attention, nodded towards the bodies. "What updates have you got so far?"

Ripping the latex gloves from her hands, she looked for a bag to place them in but when one was not available, she placed them into her pocket and picked up half a bottle of water from the sideboard on the opposite side of the room. After two long gulps she screwed the top back on and used the bottle as a prop to point out areas of interest.

"Battered like the others, although I have to admit, the injuries, albeit fatal, do not seem to be a result of as much fury as the others."

"Perhaps these two didn't run," said Watling, instantly causing a moment of silence.

Hilary raised her eyebrows and took another quick sip of water before continuing. "The rock you found under the armchair is probably the murder weapon. The gashes in the head and face and the area of the bruising is fairly consistent with the shape and size of the rock, but these are the only two that I've seen that have been attacked by a weapon such as this. There is so much damage to all the bodies I've seen that it's difficult to know which blow killed them."

"Any idea who we're after?"

"There is damage to the top of the cranium and parietal bone on both of these bodies. The tallest is Mr Brashear at five foot nine inches, so I would suggest our killer is six foot at least."

"Unless the victims were on their knees at the time."

"The force of these blows? They'd knock you off your feet. But, with the amount of injury around the lower legs, I think we can presume the killer repeatedly beat them while they were on the ground, perhaps while they were kicking for their lives."

"And the amount of strength suggests a male?" asked Watling, raising the inflection at the end of his sentence.

"A man with a lot of upper body power."

"Any trace of this…man?"

Hilary did not reply. She sheepishly turned round and looked at the two paramedics who nodded an acknowledgment before walking to her case of equipment. She took out a long purple bar and pressed a button housed on the side. A violet gleam surrounded the instrument but then filled the room with purple radiance when the paramedics turned off the halogen lamps. Hilary moved the ultra violet bar across the floor revealing what looked like a footprint.

"Barefoot?"

"Perhaps," replied Hilary. "With only three large toes and a smooth sole suggests some type of moccasin, leather maybe or plastic." She moved the bar closer to the front door of the building. "They lead outside where they stop. By the length of the gait I would say we're definitely looking at someone over six-foot tall and a confidence that allows him to simply walk into the building and commit sheer, brute force murder."

"Fingerprints?"

"Nothing." Hilary moved the U/V light up the panels of the door.

Watling's radio buzzed with static. He took it to hand and raised it to his mouth. "Hello, can anyone hear me?"

The volume of the white noise increased as Hilary drew the U/V lamp higher up the door. "You see, nothing, and we know he came through here."

There was an explosion of static from the radio and Hilary shrieked in fright as under the violet glow of the lamp, a face of pure white stared back at her through the window in the door. She staggered back and stumbled into Watling who steadied her balance. When she raised the lamp again, the face had gone and through the static on the radio waves, Cosgrove's voice emerged.

"George, can you hear me? I think this damn radio is actually working again."

"What the hell was that face?" Hilary's eyes were transfixed on the pane of glass in the door. Suddenly the face appeared again followed by the words, "Anyone for a brew?" Officer Walsh used his shoulder to open the door due to his hands holding a tray of hot mugs of tea and a bag of sugar. "No spoons I'm afraid. You'll have to make do. Why is it so dark in here?"

Hilary drew her hand across her brow and shook her head before using the U/V lamp to guide Officer Walsh to a place where he could set down the refreshments.

Watling rolled his eyes and spoke into the radio. "I can just about hear you, Merv. Any news on Aaralyn?"

"Nothing. Can you spare a few to help with the search?"

Watling closed his eyes, tipped his head back slightly and sighed. He feared the worst, he knew Cosgrove did as well, but they couldn't say it, not in front of others. He gathered himself quickly as soon as the paramedics switched the lamps back on and with a reassuring tone to his voice said, "Of course, I'll send everyone who's free."

18:50pm

Checking his watch, Watling felt the sting of uneasiness and apprehension in his stomach. He stood on the cliff's edge, the wind blustering his coat and ruffling his greying hair. It had been over an hour since anyone had seen Officer Skanthavarathan, and his hope of finding her alive was being washed away like the tide washing away their route back across the sands. The time did indeed signify the oncoming tide, for now they were cut off until the early hours of the morning unless the winds dropped enough for air support, but then, should the winds not yield and they had to drive back, he still had his doubts at their ability in traversing the rocks under the blackness of night. Mother-nature, however, was not in the mood for relenting which gave him more grave concerns, not only for their flight from this place, but also for the missing officer. Granted, he didn't know her, she was one of Cosgrove's team, but she was a police officer, one of their own, and as he stood in the dull moonlight looking over the cliff at the lapping water beneath him, he couldn't help feel empty at the fate that must have befallen her. They would have to wait until daylight to search the rocks and he hoped, assuming she had fallen, that she would not be found by one of the younger officers. From personal experience he knew it was something that you never quite get over and he did not wish this to happen to someone like young Morris.

He tried his radio again but there was nothing, not even static this time, just a hum interjected with random clicks. His mobile phone had a red cross where the coverage bars should be and so the search for Officer Skanthavarathan had to be conducted the old fashioned way, by looking and shouting. The strong wind made this even more difficult but at least with everyone having a torch he could see where people were. Watling took one last look at the lights of West Kirby and Hoylake on the mainland, a place that seemed to have edged further away ever since the tide had encroached on their chance to leave. He turned and walked through the long grass to the nearest torchlight and beckoned them to him. Cosgrove answered his gesture and repeated the word he had said far too often when they met on the island, "Nothing."

"Without radios," said Watling, placing a reassuring palm on Cosgrove's shoulder, "she could be found and we wouldn't know about it."

"For a few minutes at least." Cosgrove sighed and flashed his torch at the long grass. "She was a good kid, a promising career. How do I tell her parents? I've not had to do that before."

"You'll find the words, we all do. Let's not think about that until she's found, you never know."

They began to walk towards the main set of buildings when they were approached by the Chief Inspector. "Any joy?"

Cosgrove shook his head.

Eleanor showed little remorse. "Fallen off the edge, she has. Lost her footing, the bloody idiot. Didn't I say pairs? Make sure you're in pairs, I said. No-one ever listens. Whatever good work we do here will be overlooked by Officer Skanth… Skanthal…

"Officer Skanthavarathan," said Cosgrove.

"You see, I can't even pronounce her bloody name. That's going to look good on the news, isn't it?"

On the wind came a cry, an almost indistinct call for help.

The Chief tutted. "What now?"

The swirling gusts made it difficult to ascertain which direction it was coming from, but the beams of light from the torches of the other officers began to move towards the back of the island, towards the lifeboat station. They ran to follow.

19:02pm

When Watling arrived at the lifeboat station, there were already eight others on the scene, each one scouring the area with their torches. Eleanor arrived soon after and attempted to shout above the wind and the lapping sea that had started to foam onto the rocks. "Who shouted? Has anyone found anything?" She did not receive a response. "Talk to me, has anyone found anything? No? Okay, everyone pair up, stay in your pairs and do wide sweeps of the area."

Watling ignored his superior; instead, he walked along the cliff's edge away from the lifeboat station until he reached a place he had visited before. He noticed a torch on the ground and Watling picked it up, switching it on and off to test it. Looking down, he noticed he was standing atop the iron ladder and shone the beam of his own torch below him. His decision to extract Harry Alter's body first was justified for where he had stood earlier with Brendan and Officer Clarke was now under water with the sea breaking against the first couple of rungs. But every time the tide splashed against the rock and metal it did so with the accompaniment of a hand. Watling mouthed an expletive and crouched to allow the beam of his torch to gain extra penetration into the water. A body at the mercy of the tide's ebb and flow floated face down, its arms outstretched as if it was reaching for the ladder. From what he could see, the short cropped hair and light skin tone told Watling it wasn't Officer Skanthavarathan and that the island had now claimed another life.

20:12pm

It had taken them almost an hour to drag Officer Ashley Brenner from the sea. Three officers stood amidst the rising waves pushing the body up towards those at the top of the iron ladder who were pulling at the ropes tied around Brenner's midriff. As soon as the body was laid down at the cliff's edge, the beams from the torches made it clear that Officer Brenner had suffered several strikes to his head before falling into the water. What wasn't clear was whether he had drowned or had died before he hit the water. After the three officers had been helped back up the ladder they all stood silently, the wind howling around them, the sea crashing beneath them, their torches illuminating the battered face of their colleague, and, at that moment, they all knew they were not alone on the island. Whoever brutally murdered the six teenagers was still with them and did not have any compunction in killing police officers.

20:15pm

Watling looked at Eleanor in an attempt to get her attention but her head was dipped and her eyes seemed focused on Officer Brenner. He was expecting orders from his superior but they never came and it took his words, 'Ma'am, what about the others?" for her to break from her thoughts.

The reply he received was slightly nonplussed. "I'm sorry?"

"The others, what about the others?"

A realisation melted across Eleanor's features and she quickly raised her radio to her mouth. She swore under her breath when the familiar low hum scattered with electric clicks came from the speaker. She roughly took the radio from the jacket of the nearest officer and pressed the button.

"Hello? Can anyone hear me?" She waited for a reply, instead receiving more irregular static clicks. "Hello?" She pressed the button over and over again, getting more agitated with every second that passed. "Why do these radios never fucking work?" She tossed the device back to the Officer and finally addressed the group.

"I need four of you to carry Officer Brenner to the Ranger Station. The rest of us will check on the others and also bring them to the incident room. The danger here is very real, we need to be together, strength in numbers and all that. Whoever it is will not attack us when we're all in one room. We can then work out what our next move is. Let's hurry."

The group split into two. While four volunteers took the solemn duty of carrying the dead officer back to the Ranger Station, the others rushed across the island to the floodlit areas where the original bodies were found, hoping the fate of Brenner had not been repeated while the teams were scattered across the terrain.

20:52pm

The furniture in the Ranger Station had already been rearranged to accommodate the body of Officer Brenner, and the room was almost full when Watling entered. Brenner lay on one of the tables that had been pushed to the back of the room and Brendan was drawing a coat over his face when Watling approached. He placed a reassuring palm on Brendan's shoulder, who turned to look at him through sorrowful eyes. The noise in the room was getting louder, chatter about death, survival and revenge seeped from people's lips like a corrosive acid that slowly dissolved people's optimism and morale that, more often than not, leads to a breakdown in self-control and logical thought. The conversations were intensifying and a little worrying, for Watling feared panic would soon take them over. He wanted to calm the room but this was not his investigation. The Chief Inspector had clearly pointed that out, and, at that moment, the group needed a leader. Whether

Eleanor was the right choice was anyone's guess, but she was the highest ranking officer and the chain of command needed to be respected especially in such a demanding situation. He certainly did not want to be seen to be undermining her authority even if his intention was only to help, but he knew she wouldn't see it that way. The noise levels, however, were too loud for him to hear Brendan when he tried to speak to him, so Watling asked him to repeat what he said and leaned a little closer.

"Poor lad. One of Murphy's, Sunny, said there is massive trauma to the back of the head. He took a blow to the temple as well, which may have killed him, but there is liquid in his chest."

"His final breath was a lungful of salt water."

"One can presume he fell into the sea after being hit. Whether he would have survived had he not fallen from the cliff, Sunny couldn't say, but she did point out the damage was quite fierce."

Watling's head dropped slightly. "I think we may be in for a troubled night."

There was a slam of a door which instantly hushed the room and Eleanor stood with hands on hips, her eyes scanning the worried faces. The lamp in the corner had been knocked which altered the angle of the light across the ceiling. This caused half of her face to be shadowed giving her a stern, almost malevolent expression. Placing her hand to steady the whiteboard next to her, she used a cloth to obliterate its contents. Picking up a marker pen, she played with it in between her fingers before addressing her captive audience.

"I don't really need to tell you that our murderer did not leave the island last night. He obviously thinks he has the balls to kill one of her Majesty's officers and get away with it, well, he's dead wrong and will be caught and be answerable for what he's done. Who was the closest to Officer Brenner?"

Sergeant Eddie Carrol raised his hand, "He was with me only minutes before I heard him scream."

"And you saw nothing?"

"No."

"Nothing at all? You didn't see anyone leaving the scene? A shadow perhaps, or heard a strange noise?"

"No, nothing."

"And those whose job it was to search the island, are you sure you checked everywhere? In every conceivable hiding place on the island?"

There was a subdued murmur of agreement between the officers until Eleanor raised her voice. "It's quite obvious you didn't look hard enough and…"

She was suddenly interrupted by a voice at the back. "Unless he was under it."

The Chief Inspector's mouth pursed and her eyes glared. By her expression, it was easily discernible that she did not like being interrupted but, after a few moments of thought, she relaxed her demeanour and subtly nodded. "Good point…" she paused awaiting a name.

"Morris."

"Good point, Morris. Did anyone check for caves?"

Watling spoke, coming to the defence of the accused officers. "It was almost impossible to check for caves. The ranger didn't mention any, the light was fading and the weather was against us. To check the cliff side for caves would have put lives at risk until we had the proper equipment available and the help of the coastguard."

The Chief Inspector cleared her throat and continued. "On one hand, I want this murderous bastard caught and hung up by his buster browns, but I'm not prepared to risk any more lives. Yes, I agree with what some of you are probably thinking, we could go and hunt him down, but we've already searched the island without success, he would just wait in his filthy hole to kill again probably when one of us has wandered from the pack. He's already killed Brenner and we can assume Officer Skantha, Skant, Ska…"

"Skanthavarathan," said Cosgrove.

"What an infernal name. Yes, she was a victim of his as well. No, whatever we do, we stay together, right here in this room and wait for back up. There is no way he would even think of attacking us all together."

"Safety in numbers," said Watling.

"Precisely."

"But that's hours away, ten, maybe twelve hours if we're lucky," said Cosgrove. "Surely, there's something we could be doing."

"Our radio and phones are not working, the weather is perilous, the terrain unfamiliar, night has drawn in and we don't have a single weapon between us. Bearing all that in mind, can you suggest anything?"

Watling answered. "Our Range Rover has 3 Tasers, a couple of knives, restraints, farb-gel spray and batons, perhaps not one each but enough to take him down as a group, or at least defend ourselves before he or she attacks again."

"Who has the keys?"

Parker raised his hand.

"Who holds the keys to the other vehicles?" continued Eleanor.

Two of the paramedics raised their hands followed by Sergeant Raza and Sergeant Carrol.

"Sergeant Raza, is there similar equipment in your vehicle?"

She nodded. "All in the boot."

"Sergeant Carrol?"

The Sergeant shuffled uncomfortably in his seat. "I'm not sure, I'd have to check."

The Chief Inspector wrote 'Weapons/Cars' on the whiteboard. "No matter, Sergeant." She turned back to the group. "Now, the signal issue we're having." She placed the cap back on the marker pen, tossed it in the air and caught it without taking her eyes off her subjects. "Any theories?"

There was quiet except for the wind rattling the side of the building. "Come on," said Eleanor, frustrated. "It was working earlier, the mast isn't damaged, so what's different? What's changed?" Once again, the officers were quiet.

Eventually, Morris spoke again. "The weather?"

"Maybe, anything else?"

"Perhaps the mast *is* damaged and is only working intermittently," said Officer London.

"London and Morris, your charge is to try and get either a phone or a radio working."

"There is another thing," said Cosgrove, a little sheepishly.

"And what's that?"

"Fog Cottage," he replied.

"Explain."

Cosgrove pointed to where the building was in relation to where they were. "The place where Jessica Puce managed to make an outgoing call."

"How far away is this Fog Cottage?"

Watling turned his head and rolled his eyes. Had the Chief Inspector really not paid any attention to any of the crime scenes? His following thought of her ducking her responsibilities in regards to Operation Jackdaw in favour of a 'day out' on Hilbre Island were most probable.

"Fifty yards," said Parker. "It's literally a stone's throw."

The Chief Inspector quickly scribbled the word 'Fog Cottage' in an almost illegible scrawl and put the cap back on the pen. "Okay, what else…"

Suddenly the wind blew open the door causing it to slam against the side of the wall.

Eleanor held a palm to her chest. "Jesus Christ, that frightened the life out of me."

Parker stood up and pushed the door closed making sure the latch was securely down.

Eleanor was about to continue but turned to look at Parker. "Did you close that door properly, Sergeant? I'm feeling a draft over here."

"Yes, Ma'am."

Eleanor looked at the door to make sure it was closed. "It's weird; it's like prickling on the skin, as if spiders are crawling all over me." She shivered and regained her composure before addressing the group once more. "If you're suggesting trying to make a call from Fog Cottage then we'd need to tool ourselves up from the equipment caches in the cars, but I like the idea; but we must proceed in large defendable groups." She steadied the whiteboard and wrote 'Phones and radios'. Popping the cap back on the marker pen, she played with it between her fingers. She tossed it up in the air. "Even a text message is enough to get back-up…" Something was wrong. The pen had not landed back in her hand, nor had it fallen to the floor. Her eyes focused on the pen that was hovering a few inches above the palm of her hand. "How on earth is…" Then her neck twisted.

It was as if someone had quickly and violently wrung her throat and the sickening sound of her grinding bones caused everyone in the room to back up against the wall. The Chief Inspector slumped and fell hard on the floor of the cabin. The marker continued to hover for a couple of seconds before falling, bouncing on the floor next to Eleanor's head.

Cosgrove was the first to speak. His tone was shocked and bemused. "What the fuck just happened?"

There was silence, no- one could answer him.

The paramedic, Sunny, inched her way towards the fallen Chief.

Watling raised his palm, "Careful, Sunny."

"I've got to see if she's ok."

"Careful, we don't know what the hell that was."

Sunny reached Eleanor's body and crouched down using her hands on the floor to steady herself. She placed her finger tips on the Chief Inspector's neck, felt for a pulse before opening Eleanor's mouth and moving her own eye just above it to feel if there was any breath left in her. She looked at Watling and then at Cosgrove and before she could even shake her head to imply the Chief was dead, her body went into a spasm and then rose with force until her head fractured on the low ceiling. But she did not fall, instead, she was gradually lowered as if someone had slowly pulled her down and then held her twitching body upright. Even in the dim light Watling thought he should be able to see whoever was attacking her, but there was no- one. Just then, Sunny's face wrenched to one side accompanied by the sound of a dense, rigid blow to skin and bone. Her nose exploded red as another strike sent her head back, knocking her to the floor. As soon as her lifeless body landed next to the lifeless Chief Inspector, panic erupted in the room.

21:07pm

"Stay together, stay together," shouted Watling as the officers ran into the night. His words were echoed by Parker and Cosgrove as they followed Watling to the grassed area where the cars were parked. With the ground being raised slightly, he could see the glow of the crime scenes and the illuminated paths between them and as the cold dark of the November evening closed in on them, the halogen lamps were the only brightness on the island that acted like beacons in the gloom.

Watling cupped is hands around his mouth. "Head for the lights." He repeated his call and Parker and Cosgrove copied his cry each taking a few steps in different directions to reach as many petrified ears as possible. He knew the wind was diffusing many of their hails but he could not risk people becoming separated, he needed to keep people together and he was very quickly joined by Brendan and six others.

Brendan looked in every direction, spinning on the spot. "Where's Hilary?"

"I don't know," replied Watling, willing another wandering officer over toward them.

"It was such a mad panic, we got separated. What the hell happened?"

Watling ignored the question and surveyed the island for the closest place of possible safety. The nearest lights to where they stood surrounded the body of Graham Spence near the phone mast. He instructed Parker to access the equipment cache from one of the Range Rovers and suggested to the rest of his colleagues they move towards it for fear they would suffer the same fate as Sunny and the Chief Inspector.

In the glare of the lamps, the group had closed in leaving little room between them. Parker and Cosgrove continued to shout into the darkness both as a suggestion to head towards the lights and as a vocal beacon for anyone who may be near.

Brendan fidgeted on the spot and pushed back his balding hair. "What the fuck happened in there? George?"

Watling circled the group and went from officer to officer to offer reassurance and to subdue their anxieties, for he knew a group on the edge of trepidation were all the more difficult to control.

Brendan continued, "Who has the balls to walk into a room full of police and break the Chief Inspector's neck?" He stopped pacing and placed his palm on the back of his neck and looked to the sky. "I didn't even see anyone. Did anybody see anything?" When he failed to receive a reply, he continued his agitated walk. "How can we not see anything? What does that mean? How can we fight something that we can't see? But that's not possible, we should have been able to see him, but how is it we didn't?"

"Brendan," snapped Watling, aware that his jabber was slowly unravelling the comfort he was trying to inspirit. "Questions for another time, we need to gather people and decide what to do next."

Brendan nodded but continued his flustered behaviour.

In the wind that churned around them, rain began to whip into their eyes. Enveloped by the light the group maybe, thought Watling, but he knew they could not stay outside in the cold and the wet. They had to move to another light source. The one in the building where the two bodies were found would be the best option. It was the only one indoors and safe from the elements, and he hoped those who had not initially joined his group had made their way there. It was easier to keep morale high in a larger group that was dry and relatively warm, and it was also a place where they could discuss their next move without the twisting wind stealing their words. But his mind quickly moved to the Chief Inspector and the murderer's bold attack. How safe would they be in that building? Inside or out, he thought to himself, is there anywhere safe on the island against such brash and formidable aggression?

21:21pm

Watling grabbed Cosgrove by the arm and pulled him to one side.

"What's up, George?"

"We need to get inside, it's cold and damp out here. We can barricade ourselves in if we all move to one of the buildings."

Cosgrove nodded. "When?"

"Now."

"Agreed."

Watling explained the plan to his group and the direction they had to take. Their route would take them past the cars and then Fog Cottage before entering the ginnel at the back of the houses. Following its dog- leg, they would arrive at the door that led them to the room where the two bodies were found. It seemed simple enough and not that far in terms of distance, but as they started to move, their speed was slow as the group kept close together proceeding with caution and apprehension.

They reached the cars without incident and each member of the group aimed their torches across the landscape both illuminating their path but also trying to see if the murderer would make an appearance, for the greatest fear is the fear you cannot see and right now the group was brimming with dread. On their right, Fog Cottage emerged in the dancing beams and thoughts of trying their luck with the phone signal sprung into Watling's mind, but a killer was hiding somewhere in the darkness and he did not want the group to split so he urged them to keep following his lead as he made his way to the opening of the ginnel.

The narrow passageway was dark but sheltered from the wind. Watling led the group with his torch, flashing it over the weather worn brick, the whitewashed stonework and the uneven path. He strode quickly, remembering the same route he took in the daylight, but he stopped fast and held out an arm to prevent anyone from overtaking him. In the white glare of his torch was a body on the ground directly in front of him.

Rushing forward, he crouched next to the lifeless corpse. "Walker, quickly."

The paramedic fought his way through the group and began to check the body for vital signs.

Watling shone his torch in to Cosgrove's face. "One of yours?"

Cosgrove shook his head.

"Officer Walsh," said one of the voices in the group, "Kevin Walsh."

"Walker?"

"Dead, snapped neck," he said, lifting his head from Walsh's chest. "A couple of minutes, maybe less."

Watling stood up and shone his torch further down the passageway and then at the raised grassed area that rose from the wall to their right.

"Volunteers to carry him to the building, please."

There was a sudden crash from behind them which began nervous murmurings within the group, and Watling was about to calm their insecurities when the sound of objects being knocked to the floor started the rush. The officers nearest the sound began to rush their way down the ginnel, pushing and shoving as they tried to get through the group. Suddenly, 'Run', was their cry, and the air of agitation that was hampering the group led to the charge that followed. Watling and Cosgrove were carried along the narrow path and they found it difficult to keep their feet until they accepted their predicament and ran. Watling held open the door and hurried everyone into the building. When the last one was safe, he shone his torch down the passageway but saw nothing, no one was following them. After sliding the bolt he instructed two of the others to push the kitchen table against it. Watling then strode with purpose through the fraught group.

"Who saw it? Who was at the back?"

Morris raised his hand and Watling moved to stand over him. "Who did you see?"

"I don't know."

"What do you mean you don't know? We've left the body of Kevin Walsh out there and for what?"

Morris's nerves echoed in his trembling voice. "It knocked over the broken safety barrier and then some panels."

"What did, the wind?"

"It picked one of the barriers up and threw it towards me."

Watling frowned. "It? What do you mean, 'it' picked one of the barriers up. Who did you see?"

"No- one, it moved on its own."

Watling ceased his questions amidst the growing discontent amongst the group. As they argued amongst themselves, he noticed Hilary at the door to the conjoining room where the two bodies lay.

"I heard you shouting 'head for the lights', so myself and a few others made it here."

Watling walked past her and acknowledged Officers Clarke and Delaney and one of Murphy's paramedics.

"Have you seen or heard anything since you've been here?"

"Only your commotion, Inspector. What did you see?"

"Nothing, well," he paused. "I don't know if it was nothing or not. One of us saw something."

Watling urged everyone to barricade the windows and stay together.

"Why?" spat Delaney, "it didn't do the Chief any good."

Apart from possibly saying something about insubordination, Watling did not have an answer.

21:58pm

The large group sat in silence under the glow of the halogen lamps, fearful of the threat beyond the walls and also uncomfortable while they shared the space with the draped cadavers of Toby Brashear and Kara Winston.

Officer Delaney stood up. "I'm tired of just sitting here. This bastard has killed three of us and 6 kids. How can we just sit here on our arses, why aren't we hunting the fucker down?"

The first seed of discontent had been sown and it was followed by Officer Alston. "I wouldn't mind meeting whoever it was. Walshy was my friend; I can guarantee I'll have more than words to say to the bastard when I get hold of him."

"Morris?" Delaney walked over to the young officer, "Who did you see?"

"No-one, I swear."

"Bollocks, what are you not saying?"

Alston joined in the harassment of Morris. "You must've seen something, what was it?"

"I saw nothing."

"Bullshit," cried Delaney. "What did he look like?"

Watling stood up. "Do you really want to hunt someone down on unfamiliar terrain, in the dark, with the weather against you and without a weapon of any credibility? If you do, be my guest, the door's there, but when he attacks you by surprise because you can't see him because the rain is in your eyes, I can be damn sure you'll have wished you had stayed here to protect the group. Every life he takes makes him victorious and I don't want us to lose anyone else to this…this fiend." Watling felt himself swelling with anger.

Delaney sat back in his chair but Watling remained standing, surveying the group, analysing each expression to identify those who may require more reassurance and support, and he was about to speak when he heard heavy footsteps above him. He looked at the group. "Who's gone upstairs?"

The negative response suggested their uninvited guest was not one of his group. Watling whispered to Cosgrove, "You did check upstairs, I'm assuming."

"All over," came the reply.

The footsteps continued and Watling pointed towards the sound, following the route the footsteps were taking about the room. With a swift movement of the arms he instructed the officers to gather at the bottom of the stairs.

"Here's your chance, Delaney. We rush the room, take him by surprise."

The group nodded and followed Watling as he crept up the wooden staircase. The landing was short but when the group had only reached half way across it, the footsteps stopped. Fearing the intruder would jump through the window he charged the door, his fellow officers followed and burst into the room, fanning around the sides to surround the occupant.

"De ja vu," said Watling as he stood in the centre of the room, alone. Delaney looked out of the window and felt the glass and latches but it was secure and locked from the inside. When Cosgrove joined Watling, he turned and tried to hide his anger. "That's twice now, more fool me, eh?"

"What do you mean?"

"Ok, everyone back downstairs."

"I don't understand," said Cosgrove. "What's going on?"

Watling screwed up his face slightly. "I'm not sure, something. It's given me a stomach ache, I'll tell you that."

As they turned to leave the room, the window cracked behind them. The fractures spider webbed away from Delaney's head that was now dripping blood down his bald scalp while it temporarily rested against the glass.

Watling looked on in horror as Delaney's body contorted and threw itself against the window, haemorrhaging the cracks, sending the shards to the ginnel below. Delaney's body followed, rebounding off the top of the passageway wall into the side of the building. Watling's fragile control over the group instantly collapsed as they tore down the barricades from the doors and ran into the night.

Watling chased his colleagues urging them to stick together and shouting that safety in numbers was their best chance at survival, but his words seem to dissipate into the wind as they went unheeded in the frantic need to escape. In many ways he could not blame them, what use had safety in numbers been for the Chief, Sunny and now Delaney? Even the sense of dread was beginning to impinge on Watling as he approached Delaney's body crumpled in the narrow passageway. The lifeless, staring eyes were open and Watling crouched and gently closed them. What the hell had attacked him? He was in the same damn room and saw nothing just like with the Chief. But it was dark, and Morris running from what looked like thrown debris could easily have been the swirling wind. He stood up and listened to the voices and the commotion of the fleeing souls dancing in air around him. Was sticking together like rounding up the sheep, creating easy pickings for the person that hunted them, and that finding a place to hide was indeed the wisest option. How could he encourage people to follow orders when he wasn't convinced by them himself? Their adversary, in another bold move, had fragmented the pack once again, this time possibly for good. Was this his plan all along to split up the collective, to create stragglers and devise disharmony? If it was, it worked and now Watling felt the knot of anxiety for how many more would die before the break of dawn? He did not discount himself in that thought and almost died with fright when he felt a hand on his shoulder.

"Please tell me you have a plan B," said Cosgrove, as Watling turned with a start.

"Don't sneak up on me like that, I've had more than my fair share of frights tonight and I don't want any…" Watling paused mid-sentence and then turned on his heels. He looked at the lay- out of the buildings, pointed at the broken window and then towards the beginning of the ginnel.

Cosgrove looked at the Inspector with a little confusion. "George? What's up?"

From the narrow passageway, Watling suddenly leapt up the wall to his left and scrambled up the rising bank that led from it. He found himself at a highpoint on the island. His feet were almost level with the building's chimneys allowing for a greater view of the turmoil. As torches flicked and flashed in the distance, Watling motioned again with his hands as if trying to work something out, but it was when Cosgrove finally joined him that the lights started to go out.

The halogen lamps that illuminated the crime scenes and interconnecting paths started to explode, throwing orange sparks on to the ground. They burst one by one until the only one remaining was in the building they had just left, but within seconds, this too shattered and the dying glow in the building's windows meant the island was now in darkness. Without the light of a torch, only the dull radiance of the moon offered any chance of vision.

Watling lowered his arms and dejection filled his veins. "There's more than one."

"More than one what?"

"Our murderer is not alone."

"Bullshit. Are you serious?"

"It's the logical explanation. How can one man be behind us in the ginnel and then upstairs in the room? It's simple, he can't, so there must be two of them."

"How can we search this island from north to south earlier and find nothing?

"A good question, but not the most important question right now."

"Which is?"

"The remaining five crime scenes were all lit and the lamps shattered within seconds of each other even though they were, in some cases, hundreds of metres apart. The fact that they and the ones between them blew in quick succession is not an accident or an electrical fault, it was done on purpose by five or more different people."

Cosgrove swallowed hard. "Five?"

"So, you have to ask yourself, if we failed earlier to find traces of five people and now we know there are at least five on this island with us, how many are actually out there?"

"But, who are they and why can't we see them?"

Watling finally turned to Cosgrove. "That's a good question."

As Cosgrove uttered the sentence, "What do we do now?" the screaming started. The death of Delaney did seem like a plan to divide and conquer as the cries of pain came from every direction. The crumble of the group's sense of togetherness was seeing them become victims of extreme violence and malevolence. The number of screams and cries lingering in the dark suggested five was an underestimated guess and to cause such chaos and terror this figure could easily be doubled. They were beyond help and the only thing for Watling and Cosgrove to do now was to hide and hope they can make it to low tide.

"The derelict house, let's move," said Watling, and he bolted, with Cosgrove close behind him, down the grassy bank, jumping down into the narrow passageway when they reached top of the wall.

22:23pm

Watling and Cosgrove creaked open the back door of the derelict house and crept into one of the front rooms. It was almost pitch black and they inched their way to the most secluded corner and sat against the wall.

"I don't think anyone saw us enter," whispered Cosgrove.

"We can only hope."

It was almost a minute when from out of the black came a softly spoken voice. "George, is that you?"

Watling recognised the tone. "Brendan?"

"Thank god, when I heard you enter I thought…"

"Keep your voice down."

"Sorry. I'll make my way over to you."

Brendan was soon crouched next to Cosgrove. "I can't see anything; I had to feel my way around the wall. Do you know what's going on?"

"I think we're being hunted by a gang," replied Watling. "There may be between five and ten of them."

"For what reason?"

"For sport, fun, who knows. We've spread ourselves around the island. We're easy game now."

"Jesus."

Watling shushed Brendan quiet. There was silence at first but the creak of the floorboards right in front of them meant someone was standing directly ahead.

22:24pm

There was silence in the darkness. Watling sat motionless, his mouth dry, his fingers beginning to tremble waiting for something to happen, an act of violence on any one of them. Should he do something? Will Cosgrove or Brendan take the initiative and act? But neither of them moved. They were just as paralysed as he was. Whoever was only a couple of feet away surely could not see them without the use of a night vision device, plus, would they take the risk by taking on the three of them, assuming it was just the one person. With that last thought Watling swallowed hard but it was indeed only one person and someone they knew.

"Inspector?" said Officer Morris, are you still there.

In a hushed tone, Watling told Morris not to speak and to make his way to them. "Where have you been?"

"In here," replied Morris.

"Since when?"

"Since Delaney was thrown out of the window. Boss, what's going on?"

"We're trying to work that out," said Watling, who wanted to sound a little more hopeful than declaring the cliché, 'I don't know'. "It sounds like Brendan and you had the same idea. Tell me, did either of you notice or hear anyone else enter this building until Cosgrove and I?"

"No," replied Brendan, "We're alone in here."

"Let's just keep it clandestine for a while; we need to think as to what our next move should be."

"But, who are they?" asked Morris.

"We don't know," said Cosgrove, "we haven't seen them yet."

"They're good at hiding themselves," said Brendan, shuffling his position. "Camouflage, staying in the shadows, concealing their presence in holes and nooks. Splitting us up, picking us off one by one."

"But that doesn't ring true, does it," said Watling. "Remember Sunny and the Chief Inspector, that was right in front…"

The sound of the thud and the crack of a break was that of a hard object fracturing the facial features of one of them. In the dark, one of them let out a dying groan, but Watling could not determine who it was. He instantly got to his feet and shouted one simple command, "Run." The crunch of bone echoed through the empty house as Watling fumbled his way out of the house the same direction he came in. As soon as he reached the ginnel, he turned to see Morris and Cosgrove close behind. "Brendan," Watling, started to walk back in the house. "Brendan." Cosgrove grabbed his arms and held him back but Watling tried to struggle himself free. "I'll fucking kill them all."

"George, you can't help him."

Watling continued to struggle, "I'm going make them sorry they even fucked with us."

Cosgrove reaffirmed his grip just in case Watling let anger get the better of him. "I know, but we need to get out of here first. Morris, lead the way."

Reluctantly, Watling gave up his want for instant retribution and let Cosgrove guide him further down the narrow passageway with Morris navigating the darkness. The ginnel dog-legged again around the side and then the front of the house wherein the two original bodies still lay. Steps rose up to a patio area surrounded by a large garden and then a five foot high fence beyond that. It did not take long for Morris to scale the wooden barrier and he offered a hand to Cosgrove and Watling as they found lifting their ageing bodies over the fence a little more difficult.

They found themselves on a patch of unkempt grass which eventually led to the two brick shacks and stone cottage at the southern part of the island, the three buildings they first saw when they arrived. They had not walked very far when Watling suddenly stopped and pointed ahead of him. "The cottage."

It took a few more steps for Cosgrove to stop. "What?"

"A torch light in the window, I'm sure of it. It's one of ours."

"It could be one of…them."

"Using a torch, exposing their position? Have we seen any of them using a torch?"

Morris led the two inspectors towards the cottage and stopped at the closed front door but before they could decide on their course of action, the door slowly scraped open. Hilary quickly beckoned them in and scraped the door closed whispering under her breath as to why men have the inability to complete any kind of handy work such as sanding the bottom of a door.

22:43pm

The cottage was small, the dining kitchen in which Watling and the others now stood also contained a discreet lounge area. The only other rooms were a bedroom and a bathroom. It was obviously a place fit for two, not the group of eight which now occupied its walls. The only light came through the window at the front of the building and its curtains were shut as soon as the front door was closed, leaving them in almost total darkness. Before the curtains were drawn, Watling, recognised Sergeant Parker who was standing in the kitchen and one of Cosgrove's officers, Gareth London. There was one person he did not recognise.

"We've been keeping an eye out," said Parker, introducing himself from the darkest corner. "Mary-Jane spotted you first."

"Mary-Jane?" said Watling.

"Mildew," said Mary-Jane. "Paramedic, I came with the Chief Inspector."

"Thank you for spotting us," said Watling, smiling, even though he doubted that anyone could see it.

"We have Officer Alston as well."

"Nice to have you with us, Alston."

"Likewise, Boss. Sorry for getting annoyed earlier, sorry Morris."

Morris's tone was calm, understanding. "It's fine."

Watling raised his palm. "Perfectly understandable, but we need to remain calm."

"Have you tried to radio for help?" asked Cosgrove, his spine shivering.

"They're all still broken," said Alston, "We can't reach anyone and all we're getting is static, so we switched them off."

"Do you know if you've been followed?" said Hilary.

"As far as I can tell we haven't," said Cosgrove. "But our enemies are good at hiding, so your guess is as good as mine."

"Enemies?" said Officer Alston, "I thought there was only one."

"The times and distance between the attacks suggest otherwise," said Watling. "But without actually catching a glimpse of them, we can't actually be sure."

Hilary moved across the room and sat on the couch. "When the panic hit after Delaney fell from the window, we five just ran into the night and split up from everyone else. We noticed these buildings and chose the one with the least amount of windows."

"It's as good as any, it's quite cold though," said Watling. "There aren't many places to run to on this damn island. Easy prey for those who don't know its layout."

Hilary continued. "I don't know how long we've been here, but we've not heard anyone for a while. You are the only people Mary-Jane has seen wander this far south."

"Couldn't we just hide here," said Officer London. "You know, keep our heads down and wait for back-up?"

"Possibly," replied Parker, "assuming they don't come hunting this far down."

"I'm not sure we can take that chance," said Cosgrove. "We should at least have a plan to defend ourselves and an idea about what we should do if we're discovered."

"The Inspector's right," said Watling. "It would also help if we knew what we're dealing with. Who are these people? What do they want and where the fuck are they?" His voice was beginning to rise and he felt his nerves become agitated so he took a few seconds to compose himself before speaking again. "We should keep our talk down to whispers, speak only when necessary and we keep our movement to a minimum, let's not give ourselves away. But we need options, everyone, options."

"Have you seen Brendan?" asked Hilary, her shoulders twitching as a cold breeze seemed to brush her shoulders.

Watling wanted to keep the group focused on their survival and not have their minds clouded by sorrow or misery, so he decided to lie, and was thankful it was dark so that his facial features did not give him away. "I've not, I hope he's found a place to lie low." He was also very grateful when Cosgrove and Morris did not contradict him; obviously they were thinking the same thing.

"We don't have many options should the need arise to defend ourselves," said Parker, brandishing his Taser even though no-one could see it. "I picked up this Taser from the equipment cache. We've got one zap from this thing and that's it."

Mary-Jane momentarily looked away from the slit in the curtain and look towards the rest of the group. "The damage they inflict is sheer brute force, they are very strong. When I examined the damage to the girl in the Telegraph Station, it was severe and anyone who can break the orbit and superciliary arch with or without a weapon is someone we must avoid hand to hand combat with."

"They know the terrain and they seem to be able to find us even when we are trying to hide," said Cosgrove.

Hilary interjected, "Remember what Jessica Puce said in her phone call, ...*it's come for everyone else. Why can't we see it coming?*"

"They must have some kind of night vision technology," replied Watling.

"Perhaps," said Cosgrove. "But in that derelict house there were you, me, Brendan and Morris and not one of us saw or heard our attacker. Brendan and Morris were already in the house when we arrived, they would have sensed if someone else was in the same room, and why weren't they attacked before we even got there?"

"I thought we were alone in there," said Morris.

"Exactly, hidden, silent, how could our attacker know where to look for us let alone deliver an accurate strike?"

"Like I said, night vision," said Watling.

Hilary was confused. "I thought you said you hadn't seen Brendan."

Watling felt his shoulders involuntarily slump. He sighed and then took a deep breath. "We were all together. He was attacked in the derelict house, we had to get out of there."

"You never helped him?"

"It was pitch black, we couldn't see a damn thing."

Hilary's voice became riled "All three of you together couldn't help your colleague?"

"And do what, exactly? Fumble about in the dark and wait until we got killed as well?"

"He was your friend."

"I know he was my friend."

"Twenty years he'd been working with you and you left him to be beaten to death."

"Yes, I did and it's devouring me from the inside but I haven't got the time to worry about it right now."

"Haven't got the time? That's convenient."

Watling snapped. "For fuck's sake Hilary, wind your fuckin neck in for once. You and your self-righteous bullshit. Where were you? Did you stay by his side to make sure he was safe? No, you were cowering in this fucking shed."

Watling never apologised, neither did Hilary and the room fell to a sombre silence filled with despondency and grief. When Watling asked for options little did he realise how few they actually had.

23:39pm

It had almost been an hour and no one had said anything in that time. Watling was hoping for at least a couple of suggestions of a plan of action regardless of sensibility, but their minds must be like his, he thought, filled with fear, worry and anguish. Every noise beyond the walls of the cottage created panic and doubt. Sometimes it was the howling of the wind, yet at other times it felt like someone was scraping at the stone. Every time there was even the slightest disturbance, Mary-Jane would whisper the words, "I can't see anyone." Even for Watling, who prided himself at being laid back and calm under pressure, the thought of waiting until daybreak filled him with dread.

November 8th

"I need to take a piss," said Parker standing up. In the darkness, he shuffled his feet across the carpet in an attempt not to bump into anything and he managed to reach the bathroom door with only a bruised kneecap courtesy of the chair Officer Alston was sat upon. The feeble blush of light through the curtain in the main room did not reach the bathroom and Parker used his feet to feel his way to the toilet bowl. Of course, once the lid was up, the aim was always going to be hit and miss. It was always hit and miss in the daytime apparently, according to his wife at least, so, in a situation where visibility was zero, his urine ratio to outside or inside the bowl was going to favour the former. "We could do with a little bit of illumination in here, a black light or something," he whispered, as he tried to aim his jet onto a surface that didn't create a lot of splash noise. His whisper certainly wasn't to himself. He hoped someone was listening in the next room and indeed they were, but whereas those who heard him tutted and shook their heads, Watling sat forward and frowned, not because of the grim picture of Parker taking a haphazard leak in the dark, it was his use of the word, black-light.

118

When he heard Parker gingerly make his way back into the room, Watling said, "That's not such a bad idea."

"What isn't," whispered Parker, as he made his way back to where he was sitting in the kitchen. "Incidentally, when you go in there, make sure you've got your shoes on."

"The black-light."

Parker rubbed his damp fingers on his trousers. "But we haven't got a black-light."

"No," agreed Watling.

"But I have one in my case," said Hilary.

Watling clicked his fingers. "And where's your case?"

"In the house where those two bodies are, you know where Delaney fell out of the window."

"It's not really that far. It's just back the way we came and over that fence," said Morris.

"That's all well and good," said Cosgrove. "But apart from knowing where we're aiming our piss, is it worth the risk attempting to retrieve it?"

"No, no, think about it for a moment," said Watling, a little more forcibly. "Hilary, what did you see when you inspected the crime scene in that house? What did you show me?"

Hilary struggled to think of anything specific but finally remembered. "The footprints."

"Exactly. Whoever they are, they do leave a physical trail but one we could not see with the naked eye. They may be experts at hiding themselves, but if we can track them with the U/V lamp then we can confront or avoid accordingly."

"So, our attackers are not wearing shoes? That's bullshit," said Parker.

"What did Jessica Puce say in her phone call last night? *I've seen the Shimmer*. In all of the haste and confusion we've not actually sat down to figure out what Jessica was trying to say, because at the time what she said didn't make sense. Now, here we are in the same predicament."

"So, what is the Shimmer?" asked London.

"I don't know but what Jessica said is starting to become clearer. *It's here, it's in the room with me, I know it is*. Those were her words suggesting that whoever the Shimmer is, or are, it was in the same room as her but she couldn't see it, and so far tonight no-one has seen a single one of our enemies."

"They must look like something."

"*It's like spiders crawling on my skin*, her words again. The Chief Inspector felt a chill before she was attacked, perhaps it's their presence, the only way you know they're close to you."

"As if they give off an energy," said Cosgrove.

"Precisely."

"Enough to scramble our communications?"

Parker scoffed. "Surely, it's just a bunch of arseholes playing us for sport."

Watling breathed heavily through his nose. "We need to find a way to see them otherwise we'll never leave this island alive. Let's stop running and start thinking. I suggest we get Hilary's U/V lamp and return here."

"It's too dangerous," said Cosgrove. "We can't risk it all on just a theory, the ramblings of a dying kid."

"You're probably right, but I can't just cower here for the next five or six hours, and should the Shimmer come knocking on our door in that time, then what? We don't have any defence against an enemy we can't see."

00:35am

Officer Morris had volunteered to guide Hilary back to search for her U/V lamp. The house was not that far, it was just a short distance across a small patch of meadow, over a fence and across a garden. 'Easy', thought Watling, but the following group discussions over; which other person should go, should they all go? Should they split up? Seemed to be endless and tiresome. Deflated by the hushed bickering, Watling pulled rank and ended the debate insisting that Hilary should have two people with her to watch her back, her guardian angels so to speak. Parker patted the Taser in his pocket and agreed to join Hilary and Morris. All the others had do was sit and wait for their return.

Mary-Jane moved the curtains slightly and gave a signal when she was happy that the coast was clear, although, what Watling knew of their enemies, this did not mean all that much, but it did give Officer London the confidence to slowly open the front door. Wary of opening it too far, he left only enough space for the volunteers to squeeze through, and he closed it on Hilary's heels once she had left the building. The occupants of the cottage sat in silence; they knew their wait was going to be adorned with anguish, all the time the feeling of guilt gnawing at their souls knowing they may have sent their colleagues to their deaths.

01:09am

"How long have they been?" said Watling.

Cosgrove checked his watch, "About thirty-five minutes."

Watling stood up and paced across the carpet. "It's too long, hell, you can reach that building within five. How long does it take to find a bloody lamp? I should never've let them go out there. I should've gone on my own."

"What do we do if they don't come back?" said Alston. "How long do we wait?"

"We can wait all night," replied Cosgrove. "It's not as if we can go anywhere, is it?"

Watling was about to speak when the sound of a something scuffing the ground came from the other side of the door. Everyone in the room remained motionless, waiting for another noise, a sound to help them identify who was outside. The soft triple and then double tap at the door was the agreed code and Officer London pulled the door ajar to see the faces of Hilary, Morris and Parker. Once again, London only allowed enough of a gap for someone to squeeze through and they all quickly found a seat to catch their breath.

"Is everyone okay?" said Watling.

"Fine," replied Parker, "I think our hearts might stop beating at a hundred miles an hour at some point."

"Hilary?"

"All good."

"Morris."

"Without a hitch, Inspector."

"But, you were gone for over half an hour."

"We took it slow, very slow," said Parker. "We did a few yards at a time, deciding on which cover to hide behind and which terrain was going to conceal our approach."

"Did you see anything?"

"Nothing," replied Hilary. "No enemies, none of our colleagues, no bodies, nothing."

"Delaney and the two kids were still there, but we weren't going to start searching for anyone else."

"Did you manage to find the lamp?"

Hilary held it out in front of her letting what light there was in the room accentuate its slim design. "Snatch and grab, it was almost where I thought I'd left it." With a flick of her thumb she switched on the lamp and its fluorescent tube flickered into life, bathing, not only the room and its occupants with a gleaming essence of violet, but also the white skinned figure that stood between them in the middle of the room.

01:13am

Each member of the group scrambled against the nearest wall, the fear surging through them, their arms outstretched acting as a line of defence against a possible physical attack. The figure's movements were slight. It traversed the room as if the wind was gently swaying it back and forth as it walked, and its smooth motion seemed paradoxical to the brutality the survivors knew it was capable of delivering. It stood tall, its thick-set chest and muscled upper arms affirmed that this human-like creature was capable of exacting such violence and trauma. Under the violet glow of the lamp, its naked skin seemed to radiate a brilliant white fringed with haze of purple. It was almost ghostly in appearance, akin to an apparition of one of the dead souls lost at sea that had wandered ashore from the Irish Sea, yet it commanded a physical presence without discolour or transparency. It occasionally moved around the cottage as if it was looking for something and moving its mouth as if attempting to talk yet making no noise.

Out of the corner of his eye, Watling saw Parker slowly reach into his pocket for his Taser. As soon as the sergeant raised it, Watling gestured frantically with his hands until he gained Parker's attention. Parker lowered his arm and Watling placed a finger on his own lips to prevent Parker from speaking. He then motioned his fingers across his neck to indicate silence to the rest of the group. To Watling's right was a small bookshelf and picking up a thin paperback he tossed it towards the bathroom where no one was standing. The muffled thud of the spine hitting the carpeted floor seemed to affect his colleagues more than the creature itself as it continued to scour the room.

All of a sudden, and without taking his eyes of the figure, Watling spoke, "Two, two, tut tut, t, t, two. One, one, won, won, wo wo."

Once again, the creature acted as if it had not heard the Inspector, and in a bold move, Watling said, "I think we're looking at the Shimmer."

"What the hell are you doing?" whispered Cosgrove.

"It can't hear us."

"How can you be so sure?" said Hilary.

"Our natural frequencies when we speak highlight in the letter 'T' and the lowest in casual conversation is the word 'one', like when roadies test microphones. My thinking is, if this thing has been in this building for a while, surely it would have heard us and attacked by now. I think it's deaf."

Cosgrove pleaded. "I'm not convinced. Can we keep our voices down anyway?"

"I'm positive we're okay to talk," said Watling, sounding confident. "But please everyone, keep out of its way, it seems blind but I'm sure it's not lost its sense of touch. Mary-Jane, as a paramedic, what do you make of it?"

Mary-Jane swallowed hard and allowed herself half a step forward to look at the creature. Her voice was dry and broken but she managed to give a stammered opinion. "Erm…probably about six foot six when stood up straight, its, erm, arms seem unnaturally long, erm…" It was obvious that sheer anxiety was preventing her from getting her words out properly.

"Keep going," encouraged Watling, "It can't hear you."

"The black pupils are small but their colour could be due to the black light. Its nasal bone protrudes from a flat face but there isn't a nose to speak of."

"Hairless as well," said Hilary.

"Yes, a hairless cranium," continued Mary-Jane. "From several feet away it seems to have smooth skin, yet, when it comes closer you can see the skin moving, it wriggles and gently pulsates as if there are spiders crawling underneath the surface."

"How is it doing that?" said London.

"What the hell is it?" asked Alston. "Where in God's name has it come from?"

"Where have *they* come from," said Watling.

"Is it alien?" said Cosgrove.

"You'd expect technology with Aliens," said Watling. "Cave dwellers hidden from sight in the deep chasms of the earth, perhaps, or from the depths of the oceans, who knows?"

"Why attack us?" said Mary-Jane, "What have we done to them?"

"Hilary?" said Watling, after he saw her rubbing her temples. "What do you know?"

"I don't think it's blind or deaf."

"What makes you say that?"

"It doesn't actually know we're here. I have a feeling it knows there's something in here, that's what it's looking for."

"Explain."

"Who knows how long it's been in here with us, possibly all night."

Suddenly the creature stopped and stood still, looking at the floor. Hilary slowly approached it and held out the palm of her hand. "My hand and arm is starting to prickle the closer I get. It's as if it's giving off a radiation that reacts with our skin." Hilary withdrew her arm but stayed only three feet from the Shimmer.

"Look at it just standing there," said Parker. "I don't trust it."

"You remarked at how cold it was in here when you first arrived, that was probably our guest walking past you."

"But if it has a physical presence, surely we would've collided with it at some point," said Cosgrove.

"Not if we've been sitting here because we don't want to draw any attention to ourselves, and what if it's been in the bedroom, how many of us have been in there? None of us."

"But how do you know it doesn't know we're here?" said Watling.

"From the injuries on the victim's bodies, it all makes sense now. They were too random. If you're going to attack someone, you wouldn't aim for the calf, the thigh or the ankle, not unless you couldn't see your prey. What would you do if you couldn't see who you were attacking?"

"I'd just keep punching the air until I hit enough times," said Parker.

"Almost in a frenzy," said Watling, sighing to himself.

Parker continued. "But how come they can't see us?"

"The same reason we can't see them," said Hilary.

"Which is?" said Parker impatiently.

Hilary continued. "This is only a theory but it suddenly came to me the moment I switched on the lamp. The colour of our skin is varied, black, white, brown, olive, red, yellow and so on, but what if the colour of the Shimmer's skin is outside of our visual spectrum."

"Like ultra violet?" questioned Watling

"Or their skin is somehow covered with a type of radiation we can't see. How can we see something whose colour of its skin our eyes cannot perceive? I am guessing we'd see a haze or a shimmer because, after all, they do have a physicality, but on an island at night without illumination, we'd see virtually nothing. I believe the colour of our skin, black, white, brown and so on, in fact all colours that are within our visual range, are not part of theirs. It's probably the same with sound. There are frequencies that humans cannot hear and the Shimmer's perception of sound, if opposite to ours in the same way sight is, then it would explain why we can be in the same room and have a conversation without it knowing. It doesn't seem to have a conventional nose, well, as to what we understand a nose should be like, so, my guess is it can't detect us by scent either."

"How does it know where we are? It honed in on Brendan pretty quickly, remember," said Cosgrove.

Hilary admitted defeat. "I can't answer that one."

Watling thought for a few moments and then blurted the word, "Fingerprints."

"Oh shit," said Hilary sitting back down.

"You can see fingerprints under a U/V light just like we can see the Shimmer's footprint. What was the last thing Brendan did before he sat down next to us?"

"He said he felt his way around the…" Cosgrove stopped himself and then dejectedly said, "…wall."

Watling continued, "The Chief Inspector was touching the whiteboard and tossing a marker pen in the air, all with fresh prints on them."

"Delaney was checking the windows when he was attacked," added Parker.

"When we touch something with our fingers we leave grease, a residue, moisture on a surface that these things can track," said Hilary. "Imagine if you saw random fingerprints suddenly appear on the wall, you could probably work out where the person was just by following them."

"But that makes no sense," said London. "We've been in here for hours yet this thing hasn't harmed us."

"Have you seen this place?" said Watling, "it's all carpet, cloth and upholstery, and how many times have you actually touched something?"

Hilary interrupted. "Imagine a footprint on a beach. It makes a good impression and easy to follow, but a footprint on leaves or grass is different, you know something's walked on it but how long ago? It wouldn't be very clear as to which way it had gone. Even impressions in sand fade away when the tide comes in. It knows there's something in here but it can't work out where it is."

"Can we test that theory?" asked Watling?

Hilary nodded. "I think so."

Cosgrove rubbed his head, nervously. "What've you got in mind, George?"

Watling stood up, manoeuvred his way past the Shimmer and walked into the bedroom. He took out his torch and placed his fingers over the bulb before switching it on. His fingers glowed pink as the light tried to escape, and parting his digits by only a fraction gave him enough visibility to see a picture frame on the wall, a non-porous surface to test the theory. With careful precision, Watling reached up and placed one fresh finger print on the glass and stood back. He could see the Shimmer from the bedroom and, like the others, kept a keen eye on its behaviour. For over four tense minutes the Shimmer never looked Watling's way until all of a sudden it acted as if something had caught its attention. It stopped moving and slowly moved its head until it was staring directly into the bedroom. Unhurried, it slinked its way across the cottage floor until it was only a couple of feet away from the Inspector. He held his breath as best he could when the sensation of arachnids on his skin began to distract him. The

Shimmer ignored him; instead, it was more interested in the picture frame and eventually moved forward for a closer look. It seemed lost, as if it was expecting to see more than just the one print and it moved its head to check the wall around the frame. Watling saw his chance and began to sneak out of the room, but he stopped, frozen to the spot when the Shimmer lashed out with its arms. Its attack was not aimed at Watling but at an area around the picture frame as well as the frame itself, knocking it to the ground where the glass splintered and cracked. Watling began to back away to the lounge area where Cosgrove gave his friend a pat on the shoulder. The group remained still and silent, watching the creature which had not moved since its flaying attack.

"I agree with Hilary," said Watling, eventually. "It knows something is in there but it doesn't know what or where so it's happy to stand and wait."

"So, we can just lay low here as long as we don't touch anything," said a hopeful Alston.

Mary-Jane was not convinced. "What about our uninvited guest? We can't just let it walk amongst us."

Parker took the Taser from his pocket. "I can give it a shock it won't forget and incapacitate it."

Watling shook his head. "I don't like that idea, and we've got no idea what effect it will have."

"Who cares," retorted Parker. "Don't forget how many lives these bastards have taken already, people we know and care about."

Watling re-affirmed his stance. "I don't think you should do it."

"I agree with Parker," said Cosgrove. "Consider the amount of suffering they've caused and God help us should they reach the mainland."

Parker continued, "We know how they track us and we can see them coming with the U/V lamp. I think we should take this one down. I for one would feel safer without it looking over us."

There was a mumbled agreement between the group, and before Watling could say 'stop', Parker had fired the Taser hitting the Shimmer in the chest. The fast click of the weapon was drowned out by the ear splitting sound coming from the creature's mouth. It was a high pitched noise, a broken gasp repeated over and over as if it was hyperventilating at a vastly increased rate. Each one of the group covered their ears and winced, and it wasn't until Parker struck the Shimmer with an electric iron did the sound cease.

"Fucking brilliant, Parker," snapped Watling. "I bet they fucking heard that."

"Fuck off, we all just agreed."

"Bollocks, that wasn't agreeing, that was fucking mumbling."

Suddenly, Cosgrove shushed them quiet, and as silence befell the room they heard movement coming from outside the front door.

01:36am

In the violet washed room, the group sat in silence, their eyes looking at each other waiting for someone to speak. If Hilary's theory was correct they could stroll out of the cottage undetected as long as they didn't touch anything, but it was all still supposition. Eventually, Watling whispered to Mary-Jane. "Open the curtains."

Reluctantly, Mary-Jane gradually drew the curtains aside to reveal nothing. The shuffling outside the door still continued but to the naked eye there was not a living soul near them. Watling picked up the U/V lamp, walked to the window and held it up at the glass. The rays of purple light stretched as far as they could into the night revealing a horde of Shimmer moving around the front of the cottage. Mary-Jane turned away but Watling stared at the creatures, counting as many as he could, a task made more difficult as they disappeared into the darkness when they went beyond the range of the lamp. He turned back to the group. Fear seemed to be wrapped like barbed wire around his heart, and his face and the tremble in his voice could not disguise the fact that he was petrified. "Erm…I think there are perhaps thirty, maybe more."

The air of dejection fell like a blanket over the survivors. Yes, they could decide to lie low, hide and wait out the siege until morning, but with a swarm of Shimmer only metres away from them, how safe were they?

"Do we stay or go?" asked Cosgrove.

"We should go, right now," replied Watling, quite insistently.

"Why?" said Parker.

"Because someone's opening the front door."

01:43am

One after another, the Shimmer began to enter the cottage. Watling shined the lamp towards the door and could only watch in trepidation as the pale skinned creatures crossed the threshold. The group's escape route was blocked but, should Hilary's theory be correct, all they had to do was wait out their attention and then hope they walked away. However, there was one aspect that hadn't crossed Watling's mind or that of the others. As safe as they thought they were from the sight of the Shimmer, they had not comprehended their rage, their anger, their vengeance, for as soon as they discovered their fallen comrade their high pitched fractured breath filled the room. It was repeated by the Shimmer outside the door creating a crescendo of deafening noise, which caused Mary-Jane to panic. She tried furiously to open the window but it would not budge and banging on the glass with her fist only created an echo of her skin on the transparent material. The Shimmer now knew there was someone in the cottage.

Watling dragged her away but the Shimmer moved quickly, flaying their arms in an attempt to strike something. Their speed, coupled with their fury meant their wrath would be swift, but it was Cosgrove who received the first blow. It was a stray attack, and even though he had pinned himself as flat as he could against the wall, the fist from one of the Shimmer knocked him off his feet, and he used the wall followed by the sideboard to steady himself. He knew he had made the mistake and it did not take long before the Shimmer were upon on him. Watling watched the nose of his friend's face cave in on itself and his neck break from a vile twist before the rest of Cosgrove's body was beaten with such ferocity that the bile in Watling's stomach ran up from his belly and burnt his throat. He swallowed it back down and picked up the electric iron. Hurling it at the window, he shouted at the others to get out of the cottage but already, Officer London had befallen the same fate as Cosgrove.

The window smashed but the hole was not wide enough for them to squeeze through. Alston pushed the Inspector aside and cleared the rest of the glass. Her hands were cut and bruised but she dived onto the grass on the other side and staggered away from the cottage. Without the lamp she could not see the Shimmer who immediately set upon her like a pack of wild dogs, tossing her about like a rag doll. Watling looked at Alston's blood on the broken shards still attached to the frame and then at the disjointed remains of Alston herself. "Don't get cut, they can see your blood," and with that statement, he eased himself through the window frame and fell heavily on the ground. He quickly stood up and helped Hilary and Parker exit the cottage. Standing at the window frame, he bellowed at Mary-Jane to follow him but she was cowering at the back of the cottage too scared to move. From inside, Morris threw the U/V lamp towards Watling, who juggled it precariously before wrestling it under control. Watling held up the U/V light. They were surrounded by the Shimmer as far as the lamp's influence could muster. Morris then dived out of the window but was stopped half out of the building. The Shimmer had grabbed his leg and Morris cried out for help, holding out his arms, desperately trying to reach Watling and the others. Watling placed the lamp on the ground and rushed to his aid, grabbing his arms, pulling at them with all his strength, but the Shimmer were too strong and Morris was dragged back inside to suffer the brutal fate of the others. Watling, suddenly losing grip, fell backwards and felt a crunch as he landed. The Shimmer that were surrounding them suddenly vanished leaving only darkness.

Hilary froze to the spot. Her eyes attempted to scour dismal light as the fear inside her started to swell and tremble her voice. "Where the hell did they go?"

Despondent, Watling got to his feet and felt the shards of the broken U/V lamp fall from his backside. The Shimmer that were being illuminated by the purple radiance were now blurred phantoms hidden in the night, an ethereal threat hidden from sight, always near, always close. He hung his head and let the dying throes of his colleagues in the cottage, those who failed to follow him out of the window, chill him to the core. He could not save them, they were his responsibility, but there was nothing he could do except stand there listening to the shrieks in their final breaths. He felt destroyed inside. How could he fight such hostility, such venom? It was not long before the cries stopped. What else was there to do now?

01:49am

Parker quickly pulled a morose Watling to one side and then further south until they were clear of the buildings. Watling collapsed on the grass, his will ravaged and crushed. Hilary sat by his side, there was very little they could do. Parker remained standing, looking towards the dim lights of West Kirby in the distance. "And I thought this was going to be an easy shift with some nice scenery."

Hilary crossed her legs. "So, what do we do now?"

Watling's tone was mournful. "What can we do?"

"We could get to the cars, hide in there," said Parker. "The ambulances must have those latex gloves, you know, to disguise our fingerprints."

Neither Hilary nor Watling replied. They had a basic understanding of how the Shimmer functioned but with there being so many and without an Ultra Violet lamp, the chances of them reaching the vehicles without disturbing them was unlikely.

"Nice idea, Parker," said Hilary, rummaging through her pockets. She had suddenly remembered the pair she had taken off earlier and, after producing them, she snapped them on to her hands.

Parker strode back and forth. "So, are we just going to wait it out here and hope we don't catch our death either from the Shimmer or the weather?"

"Unless you can come up with something else."

Parker thought for a moment and then sat down, defeated. "We could do with a radio or something, play a few tunes."

Hilary scoffed. "What? With reception like it is out here?"

Suddenly, Watling sat up. "That's it. Where's Officer Alston?"

01:57am

Watling got to his feet and started walking back towards the cottage with Hilary and Parker in close pursuit.

"Alston's dead, what do you need her for?" shouted Hilary.

"She had the radio."

Parker caught up with Watling, grabbed his arm and forced him to stop. "Radios don't work here, remember?"

"Not in the conventional sense they don't." Watling started walking again and then halted when he saw the creased body of Alston on the grass. He raised his hands, stretched out both of his palms and surveyed the sullen landscape in front of him. Very slowly, Watling, began to take one short step and then another. Like a blind man moving across an empty expanse, he moved his reaching palms in one hundred and eighty degree arcs. "Stay close," he said to Parker and Hilary, who quickly realised what he was attempting and manoeuvred behind him, keeping only a few inches from each other. Suddenly, Watling stopped. "The spiders."

"Where?" said Parker.

"My right arm, I can feel them. It must be close."

Watling side stepped to the left until the feeling lessened and then moved forward once more, but within three paces he felt the sensation of spiders on both arms and his face.

"I can't go forward, I'll keep going left." However, his attempts to move were short lived when he felt the familiar cool prickle on his left forearm.

"It's not working, there are too many of them," said Parker.

"Patience," assured Watling, and with those words he felt the coolness subside. "It's moved, I'll keep going."

Taking four more steps left and six forward, Watling started to focus on the body of Officer Alston. Her broken frame lay less than ten feet away but he found himself rooted to the spot for it felt like a whole nest of spiders was starting to crawl all over his skin. He took a step back and attempted to walk left in a hope to circle what seemed like a throng of the Shimmer as the prickling skin seemed to be more intense this time. Watling's skin on the left side of his body began to return to normal indicating he had reached the edge of the group and his heart started to beat even faster when he realised he was only a few feet from Alston, but then he stopped dead. A Shimmer had moved towards him from the left hand side, his eyes could only see a hazed, blurred landscape, but he could feel its presence only inches away. He stood with his eyes closed waiting for something to happen, to be bumped or struck, but the only thing Watling felt was the Shimmer move away. His body instantly relaxed and he took one extra step left before taking the last few paces towards Alston's body. He turned back to Parker and Hilary. "Remind me never to do that again."

Parker patted Watling on the back. "Well done, Boss."

"What do we need Alston's radio for anyway?" said Hilary kneeling next to the body.

Watling did not answer straight away, instead, wiping the hair from Alston's face and closing the lids over her lifeless eyes. He unclipped the radio from Alston's belt and switched it on to a constant crackle of static. "It's the same concept as the prickling skin except the radio has a greater range, an earlier warning system than using the palm of my hands. "

"But where can we go?" said Hilary.

"The tide is going out and in about an hour and a half it may be, just maybe, shallow enough for us to make it back across the estuary."

Parker scoffed. "In the dark?"

"We know we have to get to the two eyes and then we use the lights from the mainland to get us home."

Hilary nodded in agreement. "We could drive one of the cars so far. The headlights might at least give us a little guidance."

Watling looked at Parker. "I'm assuming you still have the keys to one of them."

Parker checked his pocket, pulled out a keyring and fob and nodded.

"Anyone got another idea?" Watling only paused for a second. "Okay, let's get going."

Once more, Watling stood up and began the creeping pace across the meadow towards the vehicles with Parker and Hilary close behind him.

Navigating the random positions of the Shimmer was like navigating an invisible maze. The white noise constantly bled from the radio and it was only the degrees of volume that suggested where the Shimmer might be standing. Watling stopped when a loud burst of static caused his heart to almost burst through his rib cage. The Shimmer were moving, possibly looking for their quarry and Watling felt it was only a matter of time before one of them bumped into them. But would they recognise them? For all they knew, Watling and the others could simply be obstacles, inanimate objects to be avoided, but this was all supposition on his part and with the Shimmer moving around them it certainly wasn't an appropriate time to start second guessing himself.

As they moved closer to the flag pole, the static started to relent and they could see the fence they could traverse that would lead them back to the house where Hilary had collected her U/V lamp. Watling's aching muscles had trouble climbing the fence and needed a push from Parker to negotiate the last few inches, but his efforts were all in the ascent and not the climb down and he fell heavily onto a patch of soil. He was unhurt but the jolt had knocked the wind from his lungs, and lying on his back and looking at the grey disc of the moon, he gave himself a few moments of recovery while he waited for Parker and Hilary, taking also a crumb of comfort from the familiar but, now he realised, harmless hum emitting from the radio.

Parker helped Watling to his feet and they made their way behind the house and entered the ginnel where its high walls prevented what moonlight there was from illuminating their path, leaving only their memories and the crackle from the radio as their guide to sanctuary.

Watling slowed and over his shoulder said, "Keep your hands down and don't touch anything. For all we know, they've spotted our residue on the fence and have started to track us."

"Christ, don't tell me that," whispered Hilary.

Their progress was slow and Watling was forced to stop when his foot hit an object on the ground in front of him. He knew what it was and took a long stride over it advising the others to do the same.

"What is it?" asked Hilary, as she took her long step.

Watling tried to reply as casually as he could. "Delaney."

"Jesus." Hilary suddenly leapt over the dead body and collided with Watling causing them to fall. As they both put their hands out to cushion the impact, they knew Watling was not wearing any gloves and the crackled stir of white noise in the radio suggested the Shimmer had another track to follow.

"We need to move," said Parker helping them both to their feet. "This passageway is a bottle-neck, we need to get up onto the wall and make our way across the grass."

Watling was in agreement and panic started to build in all of them as the static grew louder, and by the time Watling had struggled to the top of the wall, the screech from the radio was almost painful to listen to. The Shimmer was in the ginnel beneath them.

Knowing the creatures would soon follow them, the survivors moved swiftly at the risk of not studying the changes of sound and volume. Without this time to calculate, they would not be able to fully discern where the Shimmer were located, and also make them vulnerable to any Shimmer that were moving. But they had made good progress and the white noise was minimal. The cars were just ahead of them and their desperate need for sanctuary, that primal instinct for survival, caused them to run and ignore their logical and calculated train of thought that had got them this far.

All of sudden the radio squealed. Watling and Hilary stopped in their tracks, frozen, but Parker started to sprint and was only a couple of feet from the car when he struck one of the Shimmer. Looking as if he collided with an invisible column, he staggered, dazed, before feeling a glancing invisible fist to the side of his head. He fell against the bonnet of the Range Rover, his eyes blurred, the pain jarring down his jaw and neck. The trickle of blood he now felt signalled the beginning of his doom which was affirmed when he realised he had used his palms on the bonnet to steady himself. Surged with fear, Parker rushed for the driver's door frantically pulling the fob from his pocket. The door was unlocked and he quickly slid into the driver's position and pushed the fob into the starting slot located behind the steering wheel. He fired the engine into life. Watling and Hilary stood motionless and the headlamps blinded them as he spun the wheels one hundred and eighty degrees, spraying mud and grass in their direction. In his flight and desperation to escape, he crashed into one of the ambulances, buckling its wheel and crumpling the arch. His headlamps were smashed but it did not stop him zig-zagging the gear stick into reverse and speeding the car to where Hilary and Watling were standing. There was a bang on the passenger window and then on the boot of the car but Parker managed to accelerate away, this time avoiding the vehicles, and headed down the short road to the small beach. Without headlights to guide his way, the mobile phone mast was soon upon him and he was unable to avoid a collision with the forensic scene of the first body they had discovered. Parker did not slow down as the Range Rover crashed through the equipment and drove over the body of Graham Spence.

Within seconds he had reached the beach but in his madness he had ignored the advice Watling had given him about the tide. Although the water had receded, it was not enough to drive a car through and when the cascade of water had finally dripped away across the roof and bonnet, Parker soon found himself stranded with cold salt water starting to leak into the foot-well. The engine had cut out and Parker repeatedly cursed, banging his palm on the dashboard as all of his attempts to spark life into the engine failed. In all of his frustration he had neglected to notice the footsteps in the water, the approaching tread of the invisible Shimmer, impressions in the water that were steady but foreboding.

02:37am

Watling and Hilary had followed the car and arrived breathless at the bottom of the ramp to the beginning of the small beach. Watling's heart sank as he saw the Range Rover marooned in three feet of water. The rear lights were flashing intermittently but they could not hear the rumble of the engine and Hilary was about to run to his aid when Watling grabbed her arm.

"No, look."

Even in the dim moonlight they could see the footsteps into the water nearing the vehicle. They knew Parker's fingerprints, his human grease, would be across the steering wheel, the gear stick, the dashboard. He was an easy target for the Shimmer. The footsteps stopped when they reached the car and it looked as if no-one was near the vehicle and that the danger had passed, but they watched in fearfulness, unable to help, and when the sound of the imploding glass frightened them both, they knew Parker only had moments to live. His flaying arms and writhing body suggested the Shimmer had a chokehold on him. The human neck could only withstand so much pressure before either the need to breathe causes death or the crushing of the bones and windpipe produces the same result. Either way, Watling felt sickened that such a fate had come to his long standing colleague.

When Parker's body had stopped moving, Hilary broke free from Watling's grasp and ran across the beach. He shouted after her and then ran to follow but she had a few seconds head start on him, quickly reaching the cold water. It was not long before Hilary fell to her hands and knees as she tried to run in the thigh deep waves allowing Watling to catch up. As soon as she regained her feet she started to wade further into the dark tide, but Watling had grabbed her from behind and they both stumbled off balance and plunged into the sea. He grabbed her by her jacket and pulled her up to her feet. There was panic and fear in her eyes, so he wiped the water from her face and moved her hair to once side so he could see her features. "What the hell are you doing?"

Her voice trembled. "They're all dead, everyone's dead."

"I know that."

"I'm going to swim for the lights."

"You'll drown."

"I don't care."

"If the cold doesn't kill you, the tide will wash you out to sea."

"What chance do we have if we stay here? Everything we've done we've failed. It's pointless."

"But we can still get to the cars and wait this out."

"I can't stay here any longer."

"Come on, Hilary, we have to at least try."

"I won't wait for death to find me. Let go of me." Hilary swung her arms, beating Watling away, but he quickly grabbed her again. "Let go of me."

"I can't let you swim out there. It's certain death."

"I said let go." She thrashed with her arms once more breaking free of Watling, but he tackled her as she began to wade further towards the mainland. He picked her up and placed his hands on her face, stroking it in an effort to calm her down. Her hyperventilated state subsided slightly when Watling placed his forehead against hers.

"Please, Hilary," he said calmly, "Let's at least try and get to the other cars."

It was then they heard footsteps in the water.

Watling lifted his head and looked beyond Hilary. The sea plunged in on itself with the regular breaches of its surface. Splashes erupted and ripples quickly flowed from each foot sized depression in the tide, each break causing a cascade of salt water to drip down the ghostly impressions of the Shimmer's lower body. Then it stopped. When the water had settled and the billows faded, it was, to both Watling and Hilary, as if there was nothing in front of them and they were alone in the foreboding dark. It looked like the Shimmer had simply vanished. But they knew it was watching, waiting for them to make their move. For if they could only be aware of the Shimmer's location when it moved the water, then the Shimmer also would only be able to detect them when they moved their feet.

Yet something did not make sense in Watling's mind. The Shimmer had approached them knowing they were standing in the sea, but why would it stop? Had it lost sight of them? If they had not touched anything, how did it know they were there? Watling thought back to his previous actions and how he caressed and touched Hilary's face to calm her down. He closed his eyes and swore under his breath.

"I touched your face, it knows we're here."

Panic rose in Hilary's voice. "No, no, no, don't tell me that, anything but that."

"I'm sorry, I wasn't thinking clearly."

"But why has it stopped, have the prints washed away?"

Watling momentarily paused. "You may be right, we could wait."

"But why isn't your radio crackling?"

Watling slowly felt his trousers and then his jacket but felt nothing. "Shit, it must have dropped into the…"

The reason why they had not been attacked was quite obvious. It was not the closest Shimmer to where they were standing and it was Hilary who saw the rush of plunges approach from behind Watling. He never managed to finish his sentence; the power of the blow to the back of his head caused him instantly to black out. The jolt of the strike jerked his head forward impacting with Hilary's eyebrow creating a wide gash that dripped blood which diluted with the water running down from her hair. Briefly dazed,

Hilary was unable to hold Watling's weight as his unconscious body fell on top of her and they both crashed into the shallows. Her head disappeared beneath the surface where she remained for several seconds with the weight of Watling's body holding her down. The cold sensation of the water suddenly refined her senses and she opened her eyes to see Watling's blurred, concussed features. She pushed at his chest so his face was no longer under the waterline, enabling him to breathe, and then lifted her own head gasping for the chill of the night air as soon as her mouth broke the surface. But in her peripheral vision she could see footprints in the water, footprints that counted to more than just two Shimmer. Without them knowing, the Shimmer had surrounded them and now they advanced on their defenceless prey. The billowing water surged and bubbled in an encroaching ring around them as the footsteps gathered pace.

Hilary knew she was not in a position to save Watling so she took a deep breath and ducked under the water. Using the sand and rocks, she managed to keep herself beneath the waves and gain a little distance between her and the now floating and vulnerable Inspector. Remaining still, she waited for the Shimmer to reach her, which they did but left her submerged body alone. Hilary was careful not to make any ripples or undulations in the surface of the water so to the Shimmer she was invisible and with that knowledge, Hilary manoeuvred herself towards the beach and away from the ambushing horde. Reaching the sand, she stood up and let the water fall from her drenched clothes. Her legs were heavy and her limbs were exhausted but the frenzy of sheer blood lust that had set upon Watling's defenceless body urged her to start running. The noise of the waves caused her to glance over her shoulder to see the Shimmer pummelling the sea. Splashes of water streamed and flew from every strike which accentuated every movement of each limb, making the attack seem even more violent. But as quick as the attack had begun, it had ended, and the sudden quiet made Hilary's heart fill with utter dread. She did not know if the Shimmer were following or even if they were waiting for her back on the island. There was only one place left to hide until the morning and hope the Shimmer would not discover her.

02:53am

The cars were parked at the top of the ramp but without a radio and an ultra violet lamp, she knew that reaching them without disturbing the Shimmer would be impossible. She also knew she did not have the courage to try Watling's trick with the palm of her hands, but, when she ran past the phone mast she realised that, on this occasion, the Shimmer were giving away their location. The incident with Parker and the Range Rover had spooked them and Hilary watched the cars and ambulances become increasingly dented and smashed. She could not tell how many of them were attacking the cars but the amount of fingerprints left unwittingly on the bodywork by her colleagues and the other officers meant they were targets, and if the Shimmer were indeed defending their own territory, then they would want to make sure the human threat had been neutralised.

Her mind was blank. She had focused all her thoughts on reaching the vehicles and hiding until daybreak, that she did not have a backup plan, but as soon as she realised this was no longer an option she stood helpless knowing her list of options was very thin. She wept and then tore away her latex gloves, throwing them on the ground in frustration. The cold wind started to bite as it chilled the sodden clothes that clung to her skin. To her left was the sea; to her right was a high wall that was the edge of the grassed area behind the Telegraph Station. With the beach behind her and the Shimmer ahead acting as if a mania had taken them over, her only choice was to traverse the wall.

Furiously kicking her legs, Hilary gained enough momentum to scramble the wall on the third attempt. Her knees had banged and grazed against the stone causing her to hobble down the slope that led to the ginnel. Already walking gingerly, it only took a slight slip on the wet grass for Hilary to fall and roll the rest of the distance and she fell into the narrow passageway, landing heavy on her shoulder. She shrieked with pain and then with fright when she opened her eyes to see the battered face of Officer Kevin Walsh. Hilary rolled onto her back, held her shoulder and wept softly. Was it all going to end like this? Her career, her colleagues, her family? They will never know what happened on Hilbre Island, all the police will find is a massacre and then another group will become cut off by the tide and the cycle will happen again. They needed to know, they must be warned not to come here and getting a message through to anyone who would listen would be a slight consolation, a gesture that would mean that all the lives lost in this savage melee would not be in vain.

Hilary grimaced as she sat upright and frantically rubbed her shoulder to try and get some blood and life to it. The technique temporarily worked and she searched the body of Officer Walsh, quickly finding what she was looking for. Getting to her feet, she held his radio in one hand and his mobile phone in the other. Sighing with relief that his phone was not locked with a pin, she pressed the side of the radio and listened for the sound that told her if the devil was near. The familiar hum and intermittent clicks accompanied her first cautious steps down the ginnel. Fog Cottage was not far.

Hilary's immediate fear was encountering a Shimmer in the narrow passageway and when her radio started to fizz and crackle she remained still. Was it ahead of her? It was impossible to tell, so she crept forward, inch by inch. The static grew louder but never piercing, but this did not make her any less wary, and even when the end of the passageway was within her vision, she continued to step with judicious intent and move the radio in a smooth arc. With Fog Cottage only yards away the burst of static and the instant creeping of her skin was an indication that a Shimmer had moved directly in front of her. Did it know she was there? She crouched down and closed her eyes, waiting for the force of a blow. Her spine shivered, her pores prickled and her heart raced but the strike did not come, and when her body returned to normal and the wailing screech from her radio subsided she quickly stood up and rushed for the cottage.

Pushing open the door, she slammed it shut and with what furniture she could find, blocked the entrance. She hoped her own theory about the Shimmer ignoring sounds that reside within a human's frequencies was correct, and it indeed seemed to be the case as she waited for almost a minute to see if the din she had caused moving the furniture had disturbed the creatures. Waking up Officer Walsh's phone, Hilary moved about the small room with the phone held in front of her face, her eyes fixed on the number of signal bars. She cursed her luck at the red cross that dominated the signal indicator but continued to search for a signal before noticing the five percent of battery power left in the device. If she did manage to find a signal, she only had the chance for one call whether it would be because the phone had run out of battery life or the Shimmer found her first. But how would the Shimmer find her? She was safe inside Fog Cottage, surely, but the radio started to fizzle suggesting they were right outside, and then she remembered throwing away her latex gloves, rushing through the door and how she used her bare hands to push it open. She dipped her head with despair as she knew it was now only a matter of time, but then Officer Walsh's phone received a message. Checking the phone she noticed there was one bar of signal. Why here, what was so special about this place? Right now Hilary did not care and quickly opened up the phone's contact list and chose the very first entry. The graphic displayed, 'dialling Abi Dumas' and her heart suddenly filled with excitement and restlessness as she held it to her ear as the dialling tone started its rhythmic chime.

"Come on, come on, come on, pick up."

The call connected and Hilary was about to speak when she heard something that crushed her heart.

"Hello, this is Abi and Stan, we can't get to the phone right now, but please leave a message after the beep and we'll get back to you as soon as we can, thank you."

The answer machine finished its announcement and its final beep was accompanied by the low battery indicator from the handset. The crackle from the radio began a crescendo as the banging on the door of Fog Cottage was like a hammer blow to Hilary's already twisted gut. There was nothing left for her to do.

03:07am

There was a whimper in Hilary's voice as she uttered the words into the receiver. "Hello? Is there anyone there? Can you help me?"

She paused, listening intently, hoping someone would pick up.

"Please, help me."

Before the banging and scratching at the door, the explanation of her experiences that she had run through in her head, her last statement as it were, was a coherent and detailed account to the happenings on the island, but now the Shimmer were right outside baying for her blood and now those words were a jumbled mess. She had forgotten where to start, and without someone on the other end of the line providing prompts and verbal feedback, her mind had obliged her to simply blurt out the first sentence she could recollect.

"You must never come here. Warn others, tell them everything and beware at night, be careful what you touch, they may be watching. You can only see them under ultra violet. God forbid they should make it to the mainland. They're almost through the door, I don't have long."

It was as if Hilary's brain had taken scissors to her story and fed it to vocal chords one random sentence at a time.

"They're all dead, everyone who came here, Watling, Bright, Cosgrove, everyone. They emerge, but you cannot see them in normal light except when you think there is something in your eye or your vision is blurred or there is a cold shiver down your spine, when you feel that, they are there in front of you. They know you're there as well, they can see the residue of your fingers, the sweat and grease from your pores."

The Shimmer were nearly through the door. Hilary knew her fingerprints were all over the cottage and she would be an easy catch, that was inevitable, but her fragmented account, her garbled witness to the massacre on Hilbre Island upset her because all she wanted to do in her final moments was to prevent the disaster from happening again.

Her voice wavered as she spoke through the tears. "I don't have long left, they know where I am and this phone has only a few seconds of power, but Fog Cottage is the only place where there is a signal, I don't know why, we never figured it out. The barricade will not hold much longer. You must warn everyone, you must not come here."

The door gave way and the furniture blocking the Shimmer's access was thrown aside. The radio burst with static and the phone line started to crackle and break up.

"They're in the room, I can't see them but I can feel their presence, like spiders crawling on your skin. Please, tell as many people as you can, tell them everything but beware at night, be careful what you touch, for if they have reached the mainland, they may be watching you."

Behind her was a sudden crash and another ear piercing explosion of static erupted from the radio. Hilary felt a powerful blow to the back of the head causing her to drop the phone. The sickening squeal of pain from her lungs only lasted momentarily before a second strike to her head knocked her over. The third hit like a hammer to her knee cap before the Shimmer frenzy began and her life ended. The phone on the floor faded to blackness as the battery finally ran out of energy, but she had managed to leave a message to somebody, somewhere. It now all depended on whether or not they would listen.

Printed in Great Britain
by Amazon